'Are you alre

'I beg your pardon

'You know. Smitten. Besotted. Betrothed.' William smiled down at her, his dark eyes dancing. It was all Jenni could do not to smile right back.

'No, but...'

'Are you destined for the nunnery?'

The man was laughing! A lunatic suggestion like this, and the man was laughing!

'No.' Jenni shook her head, and her braid swung out behind her. 'But marriage... No way!'

'But that's what I've travelled half a world to do. To marry you.'

Much of **Trisha David**'s childhood was spent dreaming of romance far from the Australian farming community where she lived. After marrying a fabulous doctor, she decided doctors were so sexy she could write a medical romance, and has since written a considerable number under the name Marion Lennox. Now her vision of romance has broadened to include romances for the Enchanted™ series, and she plans to continue writing as both Marion Lennox and Trisha David.

Recent titles by the same author:

FALLING FOR JACK
BRIDE BY FRIDAY

MARRYING WILLIAM

BY
TRISHA DAVID

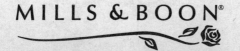

MILLS & BOON®

*First published in Great Britain 1999
Harlequin Mills & Boon Limited,
Eton House, 18-24 Paradise Road, Richmond, Surrey TW9 1SR*

© Trisha David 1999

ISBN 0 263 81672 9

*Set in Times Roman 10½ on 12 pt.
02-9905-51172 C1*

*Printed and bound in Norway
by AIT Trondheim AS, Trondheim*

PROLOGUE

'HARRIET, could you get by without me for a year?'

'Excuse me, sir?'

'If I took off for a year...? Serious question, Harriet. Think.'

Harriet thought. One of the reasons she was William's chief assistant was her ability to face trouble without fuss. Harriet was fifty years old and unflappable.

'Well, I guess,' she said slowly. 'Walter and I can cope with the administration, and you have superb chefs running your restaurants. If you were within easy contact...'

'How about Australia?'

Australia... What on earth was in Australia to attract a businessman of William's calibre?

'I thought maybe you were thinking of expanding the chain to England,' she said mildly. 'Surely England—'

'Nope. I'm thinking of a Betangera branch.' William's dark eyes twinkled at her bewilderment.

'Betangera?'

'It's on the south-east coast of Australia and has the best surfing in the world.'

Harriet pushed her glasses down her nose. She scrutinised her boss, but she was looking for something she didn't find.

William didn't seem tired and he didn't look ill. William Brand was thirty-four years old and as sharp as a tack. He didn't look as if he needed to take a year off and go surfing.

'I don't see there'd be much call for boutique hotels somewhere like that,' Harriet said slowly. 'May I ask why?'

'Why?' William gave Harriet a twisted smile, and gri-

5

maced down at the documents in front of him. 'It's probably stupid, but call it repayment of a debt. A debt that's been due for a very long time.'

'Mr Brand, you can pay off any debt in cash without having to traipse halfway around the world. For heaven's sake, your capital base and liquid assets are enormous. Of course you can pay off a debt.'

'Not this one, I can't.' William fingered the papers before him, his smile fading and his usually decisive eyes troubled. 'Or, at least, not with money. Harriet, what sort of a husband would I make?'

'A husband!' That shocked her. Over the years William had dated some of the world's most beautiful women, but Harriet had never heard he was attached to any of them. Not after Julia...

Once bitten, twice shy, they said, and Harriet could only agree. The man lived and breathed business, and, after Julia, no woman would stand in his way.

'You're thinking of marrying again?' she ventured.

'I think I must. If she'll have me...'

'If she'll have you...' Harriet gave a little chortle. 'Goodness, Mr Brand, I doubt if that'll be a problem. Most women...'

'This girl isn't just any woman,' William said slowly, still staring at the documents. 'Damn, I can't even remember her. I think I've met her. I have vague memories of a kid with pigtails and a cheeky grin, but...'

'But?'

'But I guess I just have to take myself halfway around the world and find out what she's like as a woman.' William unwound his long legs from under the desk and rose. 'Some things you can't do by proxy, and taking brides is one of them. Okay, Harriet, there are things we need to do. If you and Walter can cope, let's get this place organised so I can get myself married.'

'But, Mr Brand...' Harriet was almost speechless '...married!'

'Hey, it's only for a year,' William said cheerfully. 'Don't look so worried. I'll be back before you know it, footloose and fancy-free. You know I'm no longer a marrying man.'

'You're getting married...just for a year?'

'A year's the least I can do,' he told her. 'But I'm damned if I'll be married for a minute longer. Once married was one too many times for me.'

CHAPTER ONE

HALF a world away, William's intended bride was in trouble.

'I've won your farm!' Ronald crowed.

'Well, bully for you.'

Somehow Jenni responded with her accustomed spirit, though she didn't have a clue how she managed it. She felt as if he'd been punched. Hard. According to Martha's last will and testament, which she had drawn up herself, Jenni had lost everything.

Now what?

Jenni Hartley was twenty-six years old, her sister Rachel was five years younger and Beth was just fifteen. What Jenni earned from the farm supported them all.

What on earth could she do now?

Jenni should have expected this. Ronald had wanted the farm for years and she'd suspected he'd get it. She looked bleakly at her lawyer, and old Mr Clarins came around to press her into a chair.

'It's okay, Jenni. Let's not panic yet,' the lawyer told her, but in his heart Henry Clarins was already panicking. There was so little he could do, since Martha had not consulted him when drafting her will.

Henry Clarins approved of Jenni Hartley. Even as a youngster, she'd fought her sisters' battles, despite some pretty ordinary parenting. Then, when she was sixteen, she'd faced her parents' deaths with sheer courage.

And now defeat was staring her in the face. There were shadows under her green eyes, and her pale skin was even paler than normal. The jeans, oversized T-shirt and work boots she always wore made her look absurdly young, and her braid of thick black hair, plaited like that of a schoolgirl, made her look even younger.

She was still a kid, Henry thought savagely. Jenni was a kid with the world on her shoulders, and she'd never had a chance at being young.

'You've lost the farm,' Ronald chortled, and Henry cast Jenni's cousin a look of dislike.

'I believe your cousin understands the terms of the will without you rubbing it in,' the lawyer said softly.

'Well, it's not as if William's about to marry her,' Ronald said gleefully. 'I want her and her stupid sisters out by the end of the month. I don't know why my mother let her rent it in the first place. It'll sell for subdivision in a flash. A whole seaside resort… There are overseas buyers who'll develop the place as it really could be.'

It was Jenni's lovely farm—her dream—and Ronald would destroy it just like that.

'That's great, Ronald,' she told him bitterly. 'It'll be turned into condominiums and penthouses and parking lots, and for what? So you can have money to spend on your gambling and your drugs. You'll go through the money in a year and the farm will be gone for ever.'

'Jenni, I contacted William,' the lawyer cut in. Ronald's eyes had narrowed to ugliness and he didn't want a scene. 'There's the clause…'

Oh, yes. The clause. Put in by Aunt Martha as a sop to her conscience.

Jenni had known the farm wouldn't be left to her, but she'd hoped like crazy it might be left to William—Martha's stepson. If William owned it, then maybe Jenni could keep renting.

But Martha's stepson had left home when his father died. Sixteen years ago, William had walked away from his stepmother and stepbrother and from the farm he'd expected to inherit, and he hadn't been back since.

They'd only heard of him through the press. A few years back, reports of William's international business dealings had started circulating. William had accumulated a fortune, and the knowledge of her stepson's success had made Martha almost sick with loathing.

Thus her will today. Although the farm had been William's father's, Martha had left nothing to William—except for one spiteful clause.

'I leave Betangera Beach Farm to my son, Ronald, *unless my stepson, William, returns to Betangera within one month of my death*. If William returns, I wish him to marry my sister's child, Jenni. If such a marriage takes place within six weeks of my death, and if William agrees to live here with Jenni, abandoning his precious hotels, then I leave the farm to Jenni as my wedding gift.'

Martha's scratchy, malicious voice seemed to reach out from the grave. How many times had Jenni had to pretend to be grateful for Martha's 'charity'? 'They're my dead sister's children,' Martha had told anyone who'd listen. 'I do what I can…'

Ha! Sanctimonious, miserable old woman! And now…

Martha had left the farm to Jenni on impossible conditions, but her conscience would now be clear.

'And I hope St Peter sees right through you,' Jenni said out loud, and the lawyer blinked.

'I beg your pardon?'

'Oh, heck.' Jenni shook her head, as if trying to clear a bad dream. 'I'm sorry. I was just…'

'Just thinking about William?' Ronald leered over the desk at her. 'I wouldn't waste your thoughts. As if he's coming home. As if he'd marry you if he did…'

Right on cue, the door opened and William walked in.

William Brand...

There was no mistaking who he was. Jenni blinked and stared. She'd seen pictures of William in the press, and she had vague memories of him as a gangly adolescent, but reality was something else. Jenni just had to look at him to know why her cousin hated him.

Ronald had tanned skin and black hair. So did William. That was as far as similarities went.

Ronald was about five feet eight, and bordering on fat. William was over six feet tall and solidly built, but every inch was muscle. He had broad shoulders, a muscled chest tapering to narrow hips, and legs that were built like tree trunks.

This was a body to die for. Whew! Jenni blinked again.

The men's dress sense was poles apart as well. Ronald wore tight, black trousers that accentuated his paunch, a black T-shirt and an expensive leather jacket which needed cleaning. William wore tailored, quality trousers and a short-sleeved, open necked shirt.

And unlike Ronald's thinning hair—hauled back in a greasy pony-tail that made Jenni feel ill—William's jet-black hair was thick, short, clean and tousled, as if he'd just come from walking on the beach. He looked casual. Nice.

And William's face...

Jenni looked up into William's eyes and found herself close to smiling. William's eyes did that to people. They were set wide apart, and were open and direct, with laughter lines crinkling the edges. They were grey-black and gorgeous! His face was strongly boned. His wide mouth quirked upwards into a smile...

William smiled at her now, but it was a cursory smile—and then he turned to face Ronald.

The smile died.

'Well, little brother...' he said softly. 'Well, well.'

'William.' Ronald's voice was an appalled snap. 'What are you doing here?'

'I came home for my stepmother's funeral.' William's voice was urbane and pleasant and smooth as silk. It made Jenni shiver. 'Only to find it took place this morning.' He smiled again, but this time his smile wasn't nearly as pleasant. 'My people let me know of my stepmother's death and I came as soon as I could.'

My people...

What power lay in those two words! They implied a whole team of employees whose only job was to serve William Brand. Jenni felt Ronald's hate flowing in waves. There was no love lost between these stepbrothers. No love at all.

'I don't know why you bothered to come,' Ronald said fretfully. 'There's nothing here for you. It's not as if you even liked my mother.'

'Our mother,' William corrected him. 'That's what she always insisted she was. Replacement to my own mother. Wife of my father. Inheritor of my father's wealth. But, yes, you're right, of course. I didn't like her. Nor do I like you. I disliked you intensely sixteen years ago when I was eighteen, and I dislike you even more now.'

And then, as Ronald's eyebrows rose in query, he nodded. 'Oh, yes, I've been keeping tabs on you. I know more than you think.'

'What do you know?' Ronald's voice was high-pitched and querulous. 'What I do is none of your business.'

'No,' William said mildly. 'It isn't. But I'm wondering... Who will you turn to now, Ronald, without your mother around to pull you out of trouble?'

'I won't need to turn to anyone.'

'Oh, that's right.' William nodded, and once again it was all Jenni could do not to shiver. William's words were so ordinary…so urbane…yet there was something behind them that made Ronald cringe. 'You intend to be wealthy.'

'I am wealthy.' Ronald's sneer came back again. 'You can't stop me getting my mother's money.'

'No,' William agreed. 'I can't stop you inheriting Martha and my father's joint home and what remains of my father's fortune—though I've heard you've spent most of the money and mortgaged the house. What interests me is my father's farm. I just might be able to stop you getting your greedy little hands on that.'

'How do you mean?' Ronald's face whitened. 'You can't. It's mine.' His look suddenly sharpened into one of avarice. 'Unless… Of course, you can buy it from me if you want it so much. It's for sale for the right price, and I hear you have enough money.'

'No way.' William shook his head. He hadn't moved from his place by the door. It was as if he was here to give a message and then leave again. He didn't glance at Jenni or at Henry. His attention was only on Ronald. 'You see, I know what the farm's worth, and there's no way I'd give that sort of money to you. In fact, I'd go to long, long lengths to see you never get it.'

Then he paused, and for the first time a note of uncertainty crept into William's voice. He turned to face Jenni.

'So much so that, if Jenni's agreeable, I'll even take myself a wife,' he said softly. 'Unless I'm mistaken…' His eyes ran over Jenni, assessing her against some mental image. Against some faded memory of freckles and pigtails. His smile flared again as the mental image fitted. 'Well, well. You've grown but…you are Jenni?'

'Y…yes.' As a response, it was dumb and faltering, but it was all Jenni could think of to say. She could only stare.

It was enough. William's smile returned in full, and this time it wasn't sinister. It was even touching on fabulous.

This was *some* man!

'I'm very pleased to meet you again, Jenni,' he said softly. 'You've improved enormously since you were ten, but you're still the same pigtailed kid. But now... Jenni, how do you feel about marrying me?'

The room stilled.

Jenni's jaw dropped.

'I...' She shook her head, as if clearing a fog. 'What...?' Her voice faltered to nothing. Too much was happening too fast, and her normally quick mind was numb.

But Ronald was ready to fill the breach. 'Don't be stupid,' he snapped. The colour was draining from his face. He was frightened, Jenni saw, as she stared at both men in astonishment. Stupid or not, Ronald thought his stepbrother was serious.

But William was no longer looking at Ronald. His attention was all on Jenni.

'Mr Clarins, will you excuse us?' he asked the lawyer, his eyes still on Jenni's face. 'Jenni and I have things to discuss. Jenni, will you come with me?'

Come with him...

The last time Jenni had met this man, she'd been ten years old and William had been eighteen. She'd been a child—William's cousin by marriage, attending William's father's funeral with her parents. She couldn't remember exchanging two words with him.

She remembered her father speaking of him in the car on the way home. 'I don't know what's to become of that young man,' he'd said. 'I don't understand why his father didn't provide for him in a will. He's a decent kid, but Martha has it in for him.'

That was the last Jenni had heard of him for years. William had walked away from his inheritance, and now...

Now she knew absolutely nothing about this man—and he was talking of marriage?

Good grief!

So what should she do here? What should she make herself say?

Jenni turned to stare at her horrible cousin. Ronald stared blankly back. Fear was still on his face, but behind the fear there was contempt. Ronald didn't give a damn about Jenni or her sisters. He'd have her off the farm, and she'd be left with nothing.

But William... Marriage...

'Jenni, I'm serious here,' William said softly. 'Come with me and we'll talk.'

Serious. Ha!

But, amazingly, Ronald's white face showed he believed his mother's malicious clause might damage his chances.

Ronald's fear couldn't last long, but Jenni gloried in it. Ronald was a bully and a thief, and he'd hurt her badly over the years. If she could stretch out the moment...

So Jenni finally managed to pull herself together. Her mouth curved into a smile, her customary sense of humour resurfacing. William was clearly crazy. Marry her! It was one crazy proposition, but if it made Ronald cringe for just a few minutes it was worth it.

'You'd like us to go and buy a marriage licence right now?' she asked, and there was laughter in her voice. 'Okay, William,' she said blithely, and she rose and took his arm. It was a very wifely gesture, except her battered jeans didn't quite match William's immaculately tailored trousers and shirt—and she was about eight inches shorter than him—and she looked a country hick to his city sophisticate.

But still... William was playing games with Ronald, and she needed to join in. Let Ronald sweat!

'Let's go, then.' Jenni smiled up at William in wifely conspiracy. 'If you think it's a good idea, William...well, let's get ourselves married.'

CHAPTER TWO

THEY were a block from the lawyer's office before Jenni found her voice again, and when she did the laughter was gone.

'William, stop.'

Then, as the man beside her paused, she fought for words to say what she must. It was time now to end it. The joke was over.

'William, my truck's here. I'll leave you now.'

'Jenni, we need to talk.' William's voice was back to being urbane, smooth as silk. William was in business mode.

But Jenni was no longer in the mood for anything but essentials. The joke had passed, weariness was washing over her in waves, and all she wanted to do was to get home, shove her head under a pillow and howl.

'No.' She sighed. 'William, you've given Ronald a fright and I guess he deserves it, but there really is nothing you can do. He gets the farm.'

'The marriage clause still stands.' William was watching her strangely.

'I know. But there's no way you'd want to marry me.' She took a deep breath. 'Or me you, for that matter. I'm not in the market for a husband, so there's an end of it.'

'But...you would like to inherit the farm?'

'Don't play with me.' Jenni's weariness now was beyond belief. Tomorrow she'd have to start making plans. And to-night? She'd have to tell Rachel. Tell Beth.

Tell them what? That Rachel would have to leave uni-

16

versity? She was in her third year, studying medicine. To leave now...

And Beth... Dear heaven, Beth...

'Jenni, I'm serious here.' William's voice was sharp now, as if trying to penetrate her fog of unhappiness. 'If you have no one else in mind as a husband...well, I don't mind marrying you.'

That got through. Jenni's eyes widened.

'You're never serious?'

'I told you—I am.'

'But...why?'

The crazy question hung between them in the warm sea air. Betangera was a market town. Tuesday was market day so Betangera was busy on Tuesdays, but this was Friday. At dawn the fishing fleet went out, and at dusk the fishermen came in. The rest of the time—as now—the town slept in the sunshine like a lazy cat.

There was no one around. No one except William and Jenni.

William and Jenni and one preposterous suggestion.

'But I don't want to get married,' Jenni said flatly.

'Why? Are you already smitten?'

'Smitten?' Jenni frowned, confused. 'I beg your pardon?'

'You know. Smitten. Besotted. Betrothed.' William smiled down at her, his dark eyes dancing. It was all Jenni could do not to smile right back.

'No, but...'

'Are you destined for the nunnery? Or... You're not a lesbian!'

The man was laughing! A preposterous suggestion like this, and the man was laughing!

'No.' Jenni shook her head, and her braid swung out behind her. 'But marriage... No way!'

'But that's what I've travelled half a world to do. To marry you.'

'Why?' Jenni said again, her eyes searching his. Trying to find sense behind the laughter.

'Because I don't like Ronald.'

'Half the world doesn't like Ronald,' Jenni said carefully. 'But half the world isn't offering to marry me.'

'I can stop Ronald inheriting my father's farm if you marry me. Believe me, that means more to me than anything.'

Silence. The silence went on and on, echoing across the sea. A couple of gulls wheeled around their heads, and then veered off down to the harbour in search of something more interesting.

And still the silence went on.

'You know, I really don't like Ronald,' Jenni said at last. 'But I don't hate him.' She looked up at William and read his grim face. The laughter had now disappeared completely. This man was totally in earnest. 'Not like you. Not so I'd do something desperate.'

'Would it be desperate to marry me?'

That was a crazy question.

Marriage! Jenni had never considered marriage. Marriage was for other women, and she didn't envy them one bit. The marriages she'd seen she hadn't liked much. Her parents... Her aunt and uncle... Ugh! No, thanks!

Anyway, there wasn't time in Jenni's life for a boyfriend, much less a husband. And she didn't even know William.

'Of course it would be desperate of me to marry you,' Jenni said carefully, in a humouring-the-village-idiot type of voice. 'I don't know you. For all I know, you have ten wives already, and another three buried in your cellar. And for you to marry me... That's seriously weird!'

William's mouth twitched again and his magnetic grin

reappeared. 'Not so weird. Jenni, I promise I don't bury wives in my cellar. I'll provide character references if you like. Or let you inspect my cellar. Come to think of it, I only own a penthouse, and cellars are tricky to find in penthouses. So why is it seriously weird for me to marry you?'

'Well, you don't want to, for a start.'

'I do want to.'

'Because you hate Ronald.'

'Yeah.' William smiled again, that slow, lazy smile that made his whole face light up. The smile that held Jenni in thrall. His eyes checked Jenni out, from the tip of her battered work boots to the top of her braided head, and his smile said that, despite her work-worn appearance, he totally approved. 'I do hate Ronald,' he admitted, still smiling. 'But marriage to you won't be all that much of a hardship.' And his smile broadened.

'Gee, thanks!' For the life of her, Jenni couldn't stop a blush starting. She wasn't accustomed to men looking at her as William was.

She wasn't used to men, full stop!

'L—look, this is just plain silly,' she stammered. Damn, this man had her right off balance. 'We both know it's crazy. You expect me to fall on your neck in gratitude and race straight off to the altar?'

'Nope.' William reached out and caught her hands in his. And held them, strongly and firmly. 'In this country there's a month's legal notice needed before we can marry, so we can't race anywhere. But, Jenny, this isn't silly, and I don't expect gratitude here.'

'But...'

'Jenni, think.'

Jenni stared down at her fingers. They were held fast, and she couldn't release them if she wanted to. They were strongly entwined.

William's hand was so much larger than hers.

Jenni's fingers were work-worn, her palms calloused and her nails blunt and chipped from sheer hard work.

William's hand was tanned and sinewy and strong, and the feel of his fingers holding hers did all sorts of things to Jenni Hartley.

'Think, Jenni,' he said softly. 'Don't knock me back because of stupid scruples. I need you—and I suspect that you need me.'

Oh, heck… Think, the man had ordered, but there was no way she could think. Not with him so near. Not with him so…so darned big!

For heaven's sake. What was happening to her here?

Jenni had been independent since birth and she'd been totally on her own since she was sixteen. She'd had her back to the wall since then. She was used to fighting her own battles and standing on her own two feet to defend her sisters.

But suddenly… The linking of their hands shifted her foundations. Made her feel…

Made her feel just how damnably alone she was. Just how hard the wall was at her back, and how insurmountable the odds were.

If this man was serious…

But, of course, he wasn't.

'Don't…' Her voice faltered. She wasn't going to cry. She wasn't!

'Jenni, this is not silly,' William said, and his voice was suddenly urgent. 'I wouldn't ask you to marry me if it wasn't a serious offer. I know the farm's your home. I know…'

'How do you know?'

'I've made it my business to know.'

'But…why?'

'The farm was my home when I was a boy,' William told

her. 'I lived in it with my parents until my mother died and
my father remarried. Martha hated it and she forced my father to move into town, but I've kept tabs on it since then
and I'll not see Ronald with it.'

'It's true, though,' Jenni said slowly. 'What Ronald said.
I've read of you in the papers. You're rich. If you want it
so badly then you could buy it.'

'I won't buy it from Ronald. There is no way I will ever
give that creep money. If you marry me, then in twelve
months you'll own the farm outright. If you wish to sell it
then I'll buy it from you, but I will not buy it from Ronald.'

'In twelve months…'

'My lawyers tell me that marriage followed by twelve
months of me living here away from my hotels will satisfy
the requirements of the will. After that, we'll divorce and
get on with our lives.'

His smile deepened again. Beguiling…

'So this is not a permanent thing here, Jenni. After twelve
months you can go back to your nunnery or your lesbian
lover or any alternative you fancy. All you have to do is
stomach me for a husband for twelve months. What do you
say?'

Jenni stared. 'I say you're crazy,' she managed.

'Yes. I'm crazy.' William lifted their linked hands. He
stared down at their entwined fingers, and the corners of his
mouth quirked into a self-mocking smile. 'Jenni, Ronald is
a crooked, vicious little thug. He was when he was seventeen
and he still is.'

'But…'

But William wasn't to be interrupted. The grimness in his
face deepened as he remembered. He needed her to understand.

'Jenni, when Ronald was seventeen and Martha and my
father had been married for two years, Ronald held a party

at our home and brought drugs on to the place. My father wasn't home. I'd just started university and Dad had come to visit me. But then… Dad came home earlier than expected and found Ronald dealing drugs.'

'Oh, no.' It didn't surprise Jenni, though. There'd been rumours of Ronald's links with the drugs trade.

'When he confronted Ronald, Ronald turned vicious,' William told her. 'Dad tried to take the drugs from him, but Ronald fought. He hit him. Not once, but over and over. And my father had a heart attack. He died the next day.'

'Oh, no…'

'My stepmother swore the bruises were caused by a fall earlier in the day,' William said heavily. 'It was only me who'd seen my father that night who knew he hadn't been bruised earlier. The weirdos—addicts—who were at the party told me what happened, but they wouldn't repeat it to the police. It was my word against Ronald's and Martha's, so there was no case to answer. End of story.'

William's mouth set in a harsh line, memory biting deep. 'I don't want sympathy here, Jenni,' he told her. 'I just want you to understand. There is no way Ronald is getting my father's farm if I can prevent it. Therefore it would give me considerable pleasure to marry you.'

'For revenge?'

'That's right.' William forced his voice to lighten. 'What better reason than revenge? And you, Jenni? You want the farm for financial security? So… Money and revenge. What better partnership? It's a marriage made in heaven. All we need to do is to say till death do us part—for a year!'

It took William another hour and three cups of coffee before he talked his intended bride around, and when he did she was still full of doubts.

'William, I can't see that it will work.'

'It will,' he told her. 'We register for marriage now. We then have a legal requirement of a month's wait before we can marry. I'll use that month to set things up. I'll go back to the States tonight to sort things out. I'll fix up an office on the farm and put in extra phone lines so I can use e-mail and teleconferencing and fax. I'll work from the farm. You'll hardly see me.'

'So…you're sure it would be okay? The lawyers would accept a marriage in name only?' Jenni asked doubtfully, staring at the dregs of her coffee.

'I'll need to sleep in the house,' William said. 'I've gone into it. As soon as I heard from Mr. Clarins after Martha died I consulted my lawyers and they've laid it on the line. We need to be seen as man and wife, and Ronald will be desperate enough to have us checked. We'll be watched. But…'

His engaging grin slipped out again and held her. 'But once the blinds are down we can do what we want. Which is—exactly nothing. You needn't worry, Jenni. I don't want a real wife. I can sleep on a sofa for twelve months—as long as it's a long sofa.'

'You must really hate him,' Jenni said slowly, trying to block out the thought of William's long body on her small sofa.

'Why? How hard is your sofa?'

But Jenni refused to smile. With difficulty she managed to block out sleeping arrangements, and she stared across the table at William with troubled eyes. She didn't know this man, and the hate…

The hate scared her. To feel like this. To be so hate-filled that he'd marry someone like her…

Wiliam saw her doubt. And once again his hand closed over hers in a gesture of reassurance. Nothing more.

'Jenni, I'm not here on some vendetta with guns blazing,'

he said softly. 'I only need to get something back that I value. Martha and Ronald milked my father dry, and then they killed him, so I need to do this, but that's as far as it goes. Marry me and there's an end to it. You'll have a boarder on the farm for a year, Jenni, but you'll be left alone and there'll be no vendetta. I promise.'

'But… I don't know how someone like you could live on the farm,' Jenni said doubtfully, looking across the table at his lovely linen shirt and his beautifully tailored trousers. 'I mean…'

'I lived on the farm as a boy.'

'It's changed.'

'Show me.' William rose and held out his hand in an imperious gesture. 'Come on, Jenni. Show me what changes you've made to the farm where your about-to-be-husband will live for the next twelve months of his life.'

Marrying William. Marriage! What on earth could she tell Beth and Rachel? She hardly understood this herself.

Jenni drove her ancient truck out to the farm with William following behind in his sleek Mercedes sports hire car and the closer she got to the farm, the crazier the whole thing seemed.

Marry William?

Good grief.

And yet… This afternoon Jenni had climbed into the truck and headed off to the lawyer's office knowing that Ronald would throw her off the farm if he inherited. William was giving her an alternative.

What was the worst that could happen? she asked herself. That William marry her and mistreat her? Ravish her? Bury her in his cellar or rob her of the farm?

If he didn't marry her then she'd lose the farm anyway. And ravished?

Unbidden, the thought of William's long, lean body flooded through her mind and she had to give herself a fast mental shake. No. She wasn't exactly terrified of a spot of ravishment.

What else was she worried about? Oh, yeah. Thuggery. Well, William was no wife-beater. No one could smile like that and beat his wife—or bury her in his cellar.

How could she know that? He was capable of hate.

He didn't hate her. Not with that smile...

The thought of William's smile lingered in her mind. Jenni looked in the rear-view mirror and she could see William following. He was too far back for her to see his face, but she could almost imagine that smile still lingering.

Marriage to William... Whew! There was some toe-curling imagery here.

And the alternative?

There was no alternative.

Without the farm Rachel would have to give up university, and for Rachel to give up medicine this far through was unthinkable. And for Beth... For Beth, especially, there was no choice.

'It seems I'll just have to marry the man,' Jenni told herself out loud, and for the life of her she couldn't stop a tiny smile curving the corners of her mouth. Marriage to William... If it really could work—to be married to a man in name only...

It would drive Ronald nuts, and there might just be added benefits.

No. Don't think about the sex angle here, she told herself fiercely. Don't!

Jenni glanced again in her rear-view mirror and her smile broadened into a full-faced grin. Even without the sex bit— hey, she'd have a man about the house. A man! Jenni usually saw men as a useless kind of species, but this one at least was strong and fit. That meant…

Jenni started thinking exactly what that meant, concentrating fiercely on the external attractions. Instead of what her toes were doing, she forced herself to think of practicalities.

The roof badly needed reshingling, and so far the thought had left her feeling exhausted. She'd been dreading it. A husband ought to help with that sort of thing.

And the pigs… Every night she fed the pigs but that gate… It was so heavy and the wood was rotten. The pig gate was enough to make her want to leave the farm all on its own.

A husband ought to help there, too.

Hey, and the painting…

The farmhouse ceiling was sixteen feet high, and she got vertigo on a ladder when she looked upwards. Rachel usually helped, but Rachel was hardly ever home now. Jenni did it but she hated it. Whereas a husband…

All of a sudden she found herself chuckling out loud.

William Brand might think he was getting himself a quiet bride. He might think he'd be left alone with his fax and his e-mail and his sofa.

'But you might just turn out to be very useful,' Jenni told his reflection in the rear-view mirror. 'You might just get your revenge and I might keep my farm—but I also get myself a useful man about the house. As long as you keep out of my way when I don't want you. I think.' She shook off the vision of William's body with another effort, and her grin deepened.

'Hey, William, I might just see some advantages in being married after all. I might…'

If William had been able to hear what Jenni was saying he might have turned tail and headed back to the States fast.

As it was, he could hear nothing but the rumbling of her truck as it chugged on ahead of him. Good grief, when was the last time she'd had her exhaust checked?

Jenni was thinking that too as she drove and as her truck got noisier. Hey, maybe William could check the exhaust too—men knew about that sort of thing. But William didn't know she was thinking it.

He was too busy thinking about practicalities.

Like… Whether or not Jenni would wear a wedding dress?

Very important, that.

And suddenly it was important.

What would she look like dressed up? She looked really good in faded jeans and T-shirt.

Hey, get out of that, William Brand, he told himself strongly. Let's not think of Jenni as a woman here. That would complicate matters way too much.

This was strictly business. He was here to get himself married, keep Ronald from inheriting the farm, get himself divorced and get back to the States. Where he belonged. He didn't belong here any more. The States was home.

He turned into the driveway of Jenni's farm and all of a sudden the States didn't seem like home any more either.

William stopped dead.

Jenni had climbed from the truck to open the gate, and she was now signalling him to drive through, but William didn't move. He sat and stared…and stared some more.

He'd known that he'd loved this place, but he hadn't been home for so many years it had been like some faraway, forgotten dream. Sometimes when he'd thought of the farm he'd told himself that it was only nostalgia that was making it seem so good.

But it was every bit as good as he remembered—and better.

The house itself was nothing. His stepmother had hated it and refused to live in it and William could see why. It was a plain weatherboard cottage with verandahs on three sides. It had one, two, three additions, like three wooden elbows tacked on. His father had told him that previous owners had built an extra addition for every four kids the family had produced, and they must have had twelve.

The cottage had looked serviceable and ancient in his father's day. Now…it was neat and well cared for, but it was still only just serviceable and it was even more ancient. A good wind could knock the place over.

But the setting…

The setting where the farmhouse stood was just plain fabulous. The house was only two hundred yards from the sea. This was volcanic land and some ancient eruption had spilled rich chocolate soil all the way to the ocean. Unlike the coastal plains further on, here the land was fertile almost to the water's edge, where it became soft golden sand.

So the forest grew everywhere that wasn't cleared. There were magnificent gum-trees—ghost gums with stark white trunks and wide spreading branches. Huge ferns… The hills rose behind the farmhouse, and a creek trickled down to meet the sea. No one had cleared along the creek, and the ferns grew rampant, like a rainforest.

There were a couple of cows grazing contentedly in the home paddock, leaning over the fence to watch the new arrivals. There were chickens clucking in the dust under the verandah. A goat was tethered to the outer fence…

How on earth did Jenni make a living from this place? William wondered, and then his gaze swung to the right, past the creek, and he saw…

His gaze stopped and held.

*   *   *

There were six little cottages, set so well back into the bush that they were almost hidden. They were built as a miniature version of the farmhouse, complete with verandahs, though each was much better tended than the house itself. They were painted muted shades to fit in with the bush, and each had a name on a board outside. The boards were almost more obvious than the cottages themselves.

'Kookaburra'. 'Mannagum'. 'Kangaroo'...

They were just exquisite.

And a sign past the gate told William just what they were.

'Betangera Beach Cottages. Holiday Accommodation.'

There was an additional sign swaying in the wind under the main sign. 'No Vacancy.'

William wasn't surprised. These cottages were paradise. You could step out of these cottages, walk ten paces and hit the surf. And what surf! The beach here was wide and clean, with soft golden sand to the water's edge. The sea was a series of long, shallow swells, the turquoise shallows gradually sloping out to the blue of deep water. The beach here was as safe as houses, but along to the east it provided the best surfing in the world.

This year wouldn't be entirely penance, William thought, but then he dragged his gaze from the cottages back to the main house. This was where he'd have to stay. With Jenni.

She was waving him through the gate. William looked up at her as he drove the few yards into the house yard. She looked worried.

Damn, she shouldn't be worried. He'd just handed her this farm on a plate. With these holiday cottages already built, it must be worth even more than his people had guessed.

Someone must have been good to this girl to build these cottages. Who had built them? Martha?

Hell, no. No way! Not Mean Martha.

Was there a man somewhere? Jenni had dismissed the

suggestion as ludicrous, yet under those dreary clothes she
was an attractive woman. She certainly was…

Hell!

'Get a grip on yourself here, Brand,' he told himself
bluntly. 'Now! Let personalities…let *sex* enter this arrangement and the whole thing will be blasted out of the water
before the marriage is a month old. Because you can't stay
here if there's emotional entanglement.

'So find out what you need to know and get out of here
until the wedding. Fast!'

There were a few awkward moments to get through.

Like…how to act when you're shown through the home
you lived in as a kid—that you know so well—when you're
being shown it by the woman you intend to marry but don't
intend to get close to.

William tried for polite interest and it seemed to work.

Jenni showed him from room to room and he nodded and
tried not to make his face go tight and hard.

But Jenni saw.

'I'm sorry,' she said softly, closing the door of the master
bedroom. 'It must be hard for you. The locals say your parents loved this place.'

'We all loved this place.'

'Then you'll understand.' Jenni stared down at the
scrubbed floorboards and scuffed her boot against the worn
timber. 'You'll understand why I'm prepared to do so much
to stay.'

'Even marry me?'

Jenni's face tilted and the look she flashed him was pure
courage. William thought suddenly, she'd marry me even if
I was a total dead-beat. Even if I was into wife-beating, she'd
do what she had to.

'Yes.'

'Why will you go to such lengths?' he said softly. 'Just because you love this place?'

'If you know so much, then you'll know I have to stay.'

'My people tell me you're supporting your sisters.'

'That's right.'

'But one sister's away at university. She could get government assistance. There's only the fifteen-year-old left living with you. If you got a job in the city then she could live with you there. There's welfare to assist with her education.'

'That's right. There's welfare.' Jenni's face grew rigid. 'Only we're not on it. Mr Brand, if you don't mind butting out of what's not your business…'

'Call me William. And if you're my wife, then it'll be my business.'

'In name only,' she reminded him. 'That's all. Don't get any funny ideas about this wedding. It may suit us both, but it's business. That's all.' She paused and then said flatly, 'When…when we're married, you can have the master bedroom. I don't use it.'

'Why not?' He was watching her as a hawk watched its prey before pouncing, Jenni thought angrily, and he made her flush. Her anger rose.

'Because when I came here I was sixteen years old and the thought of sleeping in a double bed—of taking on any sort of pretence at being a parent—scared me stupid,' she snapped. 'Even though I had to do it. Take that responsibility, I mean. Also…the room was the same as it was in your parents' day. I gather Martha didn't even want the furniture when she married your dad and you all moved out. It's still set up as a bedroom for a married couple. It…it sort of seemed wrong to disturb it. So I moved into a single bed in one of the lean-tos and that's where I've stayed. And that's where I intend to stay, William Brand. Now…are there any more questions?'

'Yes.' He was still watching her. He leaned against the passage wall and placed his hands behind his back. Watchful as a hawk. 'Who built the holiday cottages?'

'What's it to you?'

'I want to know.' His mouth twisted into a wry smile at her rudeness and Jenni flushed some more. 'Call it a husband's prerogative.'

'Look, I don't—'

'Jenni, just tell me,' he said softly. 'I'm not testing you here. I'm not trying to trap you. You act like you're scared I'm going to pounce and eat you for breakfast.'

Jenni bit her lip. How could she explain that was exactly how he made her feel?

It was just too fast, she told herself. Everything had happened so fast. She needed time away—to get herself adjusted.

But William was going nowhere. 'Who built the cottages?' he asked again. 'Did Martha have them built for you?'

'You have to be joking.' That, at least, got a response from her. Jenni's mouth set in a tight, angry line while she thought through her answer, and when she spoke the anger was still there. 'Surely you know your stepmother enough to know that. Martha did nothing here. She let us rent this place on condition we keep it habitable. That was a joke to start with. I had to reroof the house as soon as we moved in. And then she watched every improvement on the place, and put the rent up accordingly.'

'But...' William frowned. 'Why did you do it, then?'

'Oh, I did it for us,' Jenni said bitterly. 'While Martha could see I was improving the place and while I was paying her good rent, then she didn't let Ronald have it. It gave her a secure income that Ronald couldn't touch. So it's meant we've had a home for ten years. And now...'

'And now you still have a home,' William said gently. He turned and stared out of the window to the cottages beyond. 'But, Jenni, you still haven't told me. Who built the cottages? They must have cost you a fortune. If you had that sort of money...'

'I didn't.' Once more, that defiant tilt of the chin. 'I built them myself.'

'You...you what?'

'I could see I'd need a decent income,' she explained. 'Even when I was sixteen I could see that. Rachel was so smart that she had to have her chance at university, and Beth...well, Beth has special needs. So...to start with I took in boarders. Backpackers mostly. Surfers who wanted a place to crash. My sisters and I slept in one lean-to and we let out the rest. Then, with every bit of money I earned— before the real costs of the girls' education started—I started building the cottages.'

She turned to face out the window with him, looking over the six little cottages that looked as if they'd been there for a hundred years.

'Remember the stables out the back?' she asked. 'They were falling down, but the stables gave me most of the timber for the first cottage. I made mud-brick pavers for the floor. I found a stove in the rubbish tip—and an old bath and toilet. You have no idea what I scrounged. The cottages are what the holiday catalogues call "olde worlde". That's because the toilets and the baths and the doors and the beds...everything in them's *olde-worlde*.'

'You're kidding!'

While William gazed out of the window, a beer-bellied gentleman wearing only bathing trunks came out of the first cottage. He stood for a moment in the afternoon sun, scratched his belly as he gazed out to sea, and then walked down to the waiting surf.

'That's Mr Haynes,' Jenni told William, following his stunned gaze. 'His wife loves this place and makes her husband come back every year. Florence Haynes would have pink kittens if she knew she was using furniture supplied by the Betangera Council Garbage Dump.'

'I don't believe it.' William turned to stare at Jenni in amazement. At this girl-woman. She wore no make-up. Her hair was hauled back schoolgirl-style and her clothes were more suited to a fifteen-year-old than a mature woman. But there was a maturity about her that belied her appearance. She had an inner beauty that told him without words that she'd never lie. 'But...who did the building?' he said faintly.

'Me. And Rachel and even Beth.'

Despite her look of absolute truth, that shook him. 'I can't believe this.'

'That's your prerogative,' she said kindly. And then she smiled, and for the first time William saw her as she should be. This was a girl's smile. It was the smile of an enchanting girl. Not the careworn woman who'd built this place from nothing. There was still a laughing kid under there somewhere. Under all those responsibilities.

She was a girl-woman and it was an apt description. She was a weird mixture of thirteen and thirty.

'Hey, I'm not saying we didn't have help.' she told him, ignoring his look of stunned incredulity. 'Mr Clarins—the lawyer we've just been to see—he's in the local Rotary Club, and he's been wonderful. He was a friend of my father's. If I got stuck...well, before I knew it he'd have a plumber out here to give me advice or an electrician to spend a few hours on the wiring, or a carpenter to teach me how to do things. I just had to scrounge the materials and there'd be someone to help me use them.'

And then Jenni's smile deepened. 'And sometimes I'd go to sleep thinking, Where the heck am I going to get a hundred yards of insulating tape? And you know what? I'd wake up and it'd be on my front verandah. This is a great local community. So I haven't been entirely on my own.'

'No.'

William could think of nothing else to say. He stood silent, stunned at the enormity of what one sixteen-year-old girl had achieved.

Hell!

From the age of eighteen, when his father had died, William had been alone. He'd fought hard. Quit the university he'd no longer been able to afford to attend. Got himself a job as a night kitchen hand and gone to a cookery school during the day. And then he'd hauled himself up the ladder of financial success.

He'd become a qualified chef and saved to buy his first restaurant. He'd turned it into a boutique hotel and then formed another. And another.

Somewhere deep down he was proud enough of his own achievements. But compared to this girl...

William Brand was a man who stood alone. He always had. With the exception of one crazy episode, nothing and no one had touched him since his father had died and that was the way he wanted it. But there was something stirring in him now that he hardly recognised.

Recognition of a kindred spirit? No. He stared down at Jenni and rejected the thought entirely. She wasn't like him. She wasn't tough. Or hard. Or emotionless.

You could read her emotions on her face as she stared out of the window. She was determined. He'd persuaded her to marry him because that would get her what she wanted. But she was as confused as all heck—and, somewhere underneath, she was still an innocent.

What sort of life was this for a woman? She was stuck here with sheer hard work facing her every way she looked.

William stared out at the six cottages and thought of the work needed to keep them let. Plus the cows to milk and the chickens and the fencing and the upkeep on this place...

Plus the fact that she'd abandoned her own schooling at sixteen.

'Wouldn't it be easier to accept welfare?' he asked gently—but then, as he watched, Jenni's face changed again. To dismay. She was no longer listening.

'Oh, no. *No!*'

Jenni was staring out at the road. William had heard some sort of vehicle approaching and stopping, and now he turned to look as well.

It was a school bus, by the look of it, and it had stopped right in front of the gate. There was a girl in a school uniform standing by the bus door, her schoolbag on the ground beside her—and the driver was carrying a big black dog down on to the road. A dog that looked as if he was badly hurt.

'Sam!' Jenni yelled, and she took off as if her heels were on fire. 'Oh, no, Beth. Sam...'

William was left to follow.

CHAPTER THREE

BY THE time William reached them, the bus was no more than a cloud of dust disappearing around the next bend. The girl was still there, though—and so was the dog. The schoolgirl and Jenni were crouched over the roadside, the big dog under their hands.

'It was Ronald,' the girl was sobbing. 'I was waiting at the bus stop, and the next thing he was there. Ranting at me. Telling me you were a bitch, Jenni, and you weren't getting away with it. And then he came closer and I thought he was going to hit me—he sounded so mean—and Sammy growled and Ronald kicked out. And then the bus arrived. Ronald disappeared and I didn't know what to do, so the bus driver brought us home.'

'Oh, Sammy…' Jenni was down on her knees in the dust, cradling the dog's head in her lap.

'He's not…he's not…' The girl's voice was fearful. 'Oh, Jenni, he's not dead? He's not moving at all. Oh, why can't I see?' The words were flung from her in an explosion of frustration.

And suddenly William did see.

The big black Labrador was wearing the harness of a seeing-eye dog, and the girl's eyes, staring hopelessly down at her injured dog, were devoid of sight.

This, then, was Beth. Jenni's little sister. The reason Jenni fought so hard for this place to call home.

Now was not the time to ask questions. Both girls' faces were frantic with fear. William knelt down in the dust and looked closely at the dog.

The dog was magnificent. He had a gleaming coat and eyes which spoke of intelligence. His eyes were dulled now with pain, but he looked up at the people around him with absolute trust.

And Ronald had kicked him...

Quickly William's eyes ran all over him, carefully assessing. There was a laceration high on the dog's hind leg, and it had bled profusely. Jenni had already found it. She was hauling her T-shirt off, and forming a pressure pad to put over it.

Which left one thin, worn bra!

William's eyebrows shot to his hairline, but Jenni was totally unaware of his reaction. Jenni was totally unaware of anything but the dog.

William swallowed and hauled his eyebrows back into order. It took some doing. 'Let's lift him a little, Jenni,' he told her. This was important. More important than cleavage. 'Lift him so I can check his leg's the only problem.'

Jenni glanced an enquiry at him, but she moved fast, trusting him instinctively. Her hands slid under Sam's hindquarters and William's did the same at his front. Together they lifted the dog a small section at a time, and William ran his fingers underneath, disturbing him as little as possible. Searching...

Thankfully, there was nothing more to find.

They laid him gently back on the grass, and Jenni shoved the pressure pad on hard.

'I think it's only blood loss that's making him limp,' William said. He laid a hand on Beth's shoulder and gripped. The child looked so terrified she seemed likely to pass out at any moment. 'It's okay, Beth. The bleeding seems to have almost stopped. He should be okay if we move fast. We need to get him in to the veterinary surgeon to get some plasma on board. I'll get my car.'

'But…' Jenni said, but she didn't have time to finish. William was already sprinting across the yard with the ease of an athlete. In thirty seconds he'd driven back, positioning his car right beside the injured dog.

'Will you carry him, Beth?' he asked. 'If you sit in the passenger seat, I'll lift him on to your lap. The warmth of your body will help him, and he knows you best. Now the bleeding's eased, it's the shock that's doing the damage.'

He took Beth's hand and guided it to the top of the car door, and then left her to get into the car herself. Then he stooped and lifted the dog. He waited until Beth was settled and then laid the big dog across her lap.

Beth's dress was blood-stained anyway. It couldn't get any worse than it was now.

Then William looked at Jenni.

Mistake.

Jenni was now wearing jeans and one worn, thin bra— and her breasts were just gorgeous!

He blinked and tried to focus on her face.

Tried very, very hard.

'Where do I find the vet, Jenni?'

'I…I don't think you can.' Jenni bit her lip. Good grief! She seemed totally unaware that she was semi-naked. Her mind was focussing on immediate need, and it had nothing to do with her appearance. 'The directions are tricky. Maybe I should take my truck.'

'You might not make it,' William said bluntly. 'Your truck's a wreck, Jenni, and the last thing you need is a break-down.'

'Yes, but I need to go. I must.'

She did. William saw that. Jenni's face was white as chalk, and so was her sister's. If Sam died…

Jenni needed to go, but the Mercedes sports car had two seats, and only two seats.

William sighed, made his decision and tossed Jenni the car keys.

'You go, then,' he told her. 'I'll stay here and mind the farm.'

'You will?' Jenni grabbed the keys like a lifeline, but then looked down at them with doubt. 'William, I've never driven a car like this.'

'It's about time you learned,' he said, striving to make his voice light. It'd help a whole heap if Jenni weren't almost naked from the waist up. 'If you're my affianced wife then what's mine is yours.'

'William…'

'Just go, Jenni,' he told her. And then he grinned as Jenni took two steps towards the car. 'Jenni…'

'Yes?'

'Haven't you forgotten something?'

'What?'

His grin deepened. This was some crazy woman. He hauled off his shirt and handed it over.

'You're an engaged woman now,' he told her. 'No advertising.' He looked pointedly at her wonderful cleavage.

Jenni stared down, following his gaze—and finally she realised. And she blushed bright crimson.

'Just get going,' he told her as she made a grab for his shirt and clutched it across her breasts, but then he hesitated as a small boy came tearing across the yard.

'Jenni, come quick,' the child was yelling. 'Dad says I have to tell you… I opened the pig's gate for a look at the piglets and now I can't get it closed again. And the pigs are going everywhere.'

'Oh, help…' Jenni paused and looked out towards the pigsty, clearly torn.

But William was pressing her down into the driver's seat.

'Just go, Jenni,' he told her. 'Leave the farm to me. And the pigs. Trust me. Just go.'

It was five hours later before Jenni finally made it back to the farm, and the little car was loaded to the Plimsoll Line.

They'd left Sam at the vet's. Beth and Jenni had watched the vet set up a drip and had waited until Sam had shown signs that he'd make it. The plasma had worked.

'It was only blood loss that did the damage,' the vet said. 'Now we're restoring his fluid balance and he's recovering from shock he'll be fine. Leave him with me overnight and I'll keep the drip running. Telephone me in the morning to check that I'm right, but I see no reason why you shouldn't have him home by lunchtime.'

Beth bade her dog a tearful farewell and, three hours after they'd arrived, they were standing outside the vet's wondering what to do next.

Next stop was the police station. Shock giving way to anger, Beth insisted they report Ronald's attack.

It was useless. There was nothing the police could do. The police knew Ronald well, and there was nothing they'd have liked better than to charge him, but it was impossible.

'I'm sorry, miss,' they told Beth sympathetically. 'But you're the only witness and…well…'

And, well, Beth was blind. One blind witness. Jenni cringed inwardly for her sister, but there was nothing more to be said.

But that's one more I owe Ronald, Jenni thought grimly. Okay, I will marry you, William. I'm starting to hate Ronald almost as much as you do.

Maybe this marriage could work. They had so much in common. Mutual hate of Ronald…

Then Jenni remembered Rachel.

Her sister was coming home this weekend and her train was due in at nine. That was in an hour's time.

Jenni hardly had time to take Beth home and come back to town to fetch Rachel. So... Could William keep the farm going until they returned? And how would they all fit into the Mercedes?

They'd just have to squash.

So Jenni and Beth had a pub meal while Jenni watched the colour creep back into Beth's face, and the life come back into her voice. The meal by themselves had been a good decision. By the time Rachel arrived, Beth was almost back to her normal self.

'And if you can't make Jenni tell me what on earth is going on, then I'll scream,' Beth told Rachel as they met her off the train and finished telling her about Sam. 'She goes to hear Martha's will, and comes home with a man with the sexiest voice I've ever heard. And his car... Rachel, wait until you see his car! It feels like you're sitting in the world's most sumptuous lounge chair!'

Maybe not—especially since they travelled home with Beth sitting on Rachel's lap. Rachel didn't travel light and, squashed underneath Beth and her baggage, she could hardly speak—but she managed a few pertinent questions. Rachel was good at questions.

Like... 'Who exactly is William Brand?'

Jenni told her. She was concentrating fiercely on not crashing William's car and she was watching out for police at the same time—they were illegally loaded to say the least—and concentration helped to give unemotional answers to questions she didn't feel the least unemotional about. 'William is Ronald's stepbrother,' she said.

'But...he's not like Ronald.'

'No. He's not like Ronald.'

'If he's Ronald's stepbrother, does that mean he's our cousin?'

'Martha was our aunt but she was only William's step-mother. So, no, he's not our cousin.'

'Then why has he come to the farm?'

'To stay for a while. To get acquainted.' Jenni took a deep breath. 'Rachel, tell me about your exams. Are you ready? Do you think you'll do okay?'

'Rach, William called Jenni his affianced wife,' Beth cut in, ignoring Jenni's attempt at distraction but muffled by baggage. 'Make her tell you what that means, Rach.'

Rachel twisted underneath Beth to stare across at Jenni.

'Yeah? Affianced wife? He called you that? So what does that mean, exactly?'

'I guess...' Try for lightness here, Jenni told herself, her fingers clenching the wheel so hard they turned white. 'I guess that means I'm his affianced wife.'

Silence. Both sisters took this on board and chewed it around.

'Affianced as in engaged to be married?' Rachel asked at last.

'That's the one.'

'So...when exactly did you meet this man?'

'When I was ten.'

'And after that?'

'Well...this afternoon.'

'And you fell madly in love across Martha's grave?'

'Across Henry Clarins' desk, actually,' Jenni said, and grinned.

'Oh, yeah...' Rachel gave an indignant bounce and Beth yelped. 'Sorry, Beth. But it's as much to try the patience of a saint.'

'Don't mind me,' Beth said faintly. 'Bounce all you like,

Rach. I'll just go through William's roof here. Just get it out
of her. Jenni, tell us!'

There was nothing for it but the truth.

So Jenni told them, as the lovely little sports car devoured
the miles between the town and home, and at the end of the
story you could have heard a pin drop.

'Jenni, you can't do it,' Rachel breathed at last. 'You
can't.'

'Don't say that until you've met him,' Beth pleaded.
'Rachel, he's something else! He didn't even treat me like
a moron because I'm blind. You know how people push me
into cars like they think I'm cardboard. Stiff and totally stupid. It was the first time William ever met me and he still
acted like I could do it. And he trusted me with Sam. He
didn't even ask if I'd be okay. He expected me to cope. He's
great, Rach.'

'You've only met him for two minutes,' Rachel told her.

'Two minutes is enough.'

'Look, we're talking about marriage here,' Rachel retorted. Jenni was ignored now. Her two younger sisters were
off in battle. 'You don't marry someone you've met once in
your life before.'

'It's only for a year,' Beth said stubbornly. 'And Jenni's
too old to meet anyone else. She's hardly likely to get any
other offers at *her* age.'

'Gee, thanks,' Jenni said, but she was still ignored.

'You don't marry someone for a year,' Rachel said stubbornly. 'What about property settlements and things like
that? Even if Jenni does inherit the farm... He can probably
claim half of it as a divorce settlement.'

'Then Jenni can claim half his worldly goods, too,' Beth
said gleefully. 'Have you thought about that, Jen?' She gave
an extravagant sigh. 'Half this car would be okay. We need

one extra seat, though. Or maybe two so Sam can join in. A great big Mercedes limo…'

'Half William Brand's goods would run to a bit more than a Mercedes limo.' Rachel paused, thoughtful. 'Hey, Jen, that's not a bad idea. We could do really well out of this. What do you reckon?'

'I don't reckon anything,' Jenni said tightly. 'I'm so confused I don't reckon anything at all.'

At least she was home. Jenni turned the car into the driveway of the farm and paused while Rachel opened the gate. Every light in the house was on. William, then, was still here and here in force.

Did he know about electricity bills? she demanded of herself, and then gave a rueful grin. Of course he didn't. Business tycoons didn't have to worry about the twenty-cents-an-hour cost of leaving on lights.

He'd have to worry about it this year, she told herself. If William was staying for a year, there were things he'd just have to learn.

There were things he was learning already.

For William, it had been a very long five hours. Possibly it had been one of the longest five-hour periods he'd ever spent. He heard the little sports car turn into the gate with nothing but relief.

He'd telephoned the veterinarian and had heard Sam's progress report. That had been an hour ago, the girls had already left the vet's, and the thought of what Jenni and Beth were doing for so long in the sports car had his relief for Sam overtaken by worry.

Jenni wasn't accustomed to driving such a powerful car. If anything happened to her now…

If anything happened to Jenni, his nice little plan for revenge would be dead in the water, but in fact it was more than his plans that had him worried.

The thought of Jenni injured…

This was crazy. He'd only known the woman for half a day.

He'd been too busy to have much time to worry, but the worry had stayed there all the time, and when he heard the sports car turn into the drive he walked out to meet it with real relief.

And watched, stunned, as it unloaded itself.

Suitcases emerged, followed by a hockey stick. There were piles of textbooks. There were legs, legs and more legs…

Finally he had all the legs sorted into order. They belonged to three young women, all in various stages of disarray.

Beth was in a blood-stained school dress. She had curly hair down to her shoulders, big green eyes like her sister's, and her face was pale with weariness.

Rachel was next. This must be Rachel. The newcomer was taller than Jenni, with a mischievous smile and the carefree look of a university student. She was wearing crushed jeans and a halter-necked top that left her midriff bare. Her hair was long and blonde, with a purple streak down the centre.

And that left Jenni.

Jenni was wearing blood-spattered jeans and his shirt which was way too big. It reached her knees. Jenni was pushing her errant curls out of her eyes—her braid was coming unstuck—and shoving the goat's nose out of Rachel's textbooks.

'No, you don't want to eat *Gray's Anatomy*, you stupid creature.' And… 'Why is the goat in the house yard?' she asked, and William grinned and strolled down to pick up a few tons of gear.

'He's a dangerous animal,' he said mildly. 'He grabbed Mrs Pilkington's beach coat and she screamed like he'd done murder. It was either bring him in from the road and pretend he's in solitary confinement on bread and water, or have her call out the armed forces.'

'Oh…' Jenni frowned as she took this in. 'I see. Does that mean we have to pay for a beach coat?'

'I already did,' William told her. 'And I apologised profusely for Herbert here. He would have apologised himself but he was too full of towelling.'

But Jenni didn't smile. 'There goes the weekend's profits.' She sighed. 'And don't tell me. You turned on all the inside lights because you're afraid of the dark.'

William turned and looked up at the house in surprise. 'The lights?'

'Every light is on,' Jenni said patiently.

'That's because it's night-time,' he said, just as patiently, and Beth giggled at his humour-the-idiot tone.

William turned to Beth then. 'I hear Sam's okay, Beth,' he told her. 'I rang the vet an hour ago and he said to tell you Sam's had some dinner and is feeling much better. He said he'll be fine to come home tomorrow.'

'Oh, that's great…'

'Is this your other sister?'

'Oh…' Clearly, Beth wasn't accustomed to being addressed as someone of importance, or addressed instead of her sisters. She half turned towards Jenni—and then caught herself.

'Oh. Yes. This is Rachel. We stayed to meet her off the train.'

'And how did you all fit in my car?'

Beth giggled again, and Jenni stared. Was this her normally painfully shy sister? Beth was bubbly enough within her family, but she was usually quiet with strangers.

'My head's made a dent in your car roof,' Beth said. 'And I can't tell you where Rachel's hockey stick ended up. I can only tell you that it hurt.'

But Jenni was no longer listening. She'd turned and was staring at the house, and she was staring with apprehension written right across her face.

'William, there's a noise,' she said faintly. 'There's a noise coming from inside the house.'

'Oh, yes.' William was at his most urbane. 'That's our guests.'

They all turned to stare at William.

'Guests?' said Rachel.

'It sounds like animals,' Jenni said, in a voice of deep foreboding. 'It sounds like pigs.'

William nodded knowledgeably. 'I expect that's because it *is* pigs.'

'You didn't...'

'I couldn't shut the gate,' he said plaintively. 'No one can shut that gate. Edward Herring, aged eight, managed to open it and the boy has better muscles than me. So the pigs got out. It took Samantha Herring, aged six, Mr and Mrs Herring, Mr and Mrs Pilkinton of beach-robe fame and the entire Haynes clan to round up ten pigs and who knows how many piglets. We've had two hours of piglet-chasing—'

'Sixteen,' Beth said anxiously. 'There should be sixteen piglets.'

'I caught twenty-five piglets.' William's voice implied that if he never saw another piglet it wouldn't worry him a bit. And then he grinned at Beth's look of confusion.

'Some were better at escaping than others,' he explained. 'I'd swear I caught the same piglet six times. We tried making them go back into the sty but the gate wouldn't work.

The wood around the hinge is rotten and, short of hacking it off with an axe, I couldn't move it. Then there was nothing to block it with. Short of knocking a few timbers off the house or chopping down a tree or two, we had to find alternative accommodation.'

'Jenni uses house timber,' Rachel told him darkly. 'Once I lost the whole wall of my bedroom because one of the guest cottages was leaking. It stayed that way for a month until we could afford new timber. Jenni's ideas of air-conditioning leave a lot to be desired.'

'William, where are they now?' Jenni's voice was carefully controlled as she ignored Rachel's interjection. She could hear where it sounded as if the pigs were housed, and she wasn't the least sure she wanted to know for certain.

'They're in the last lean-to.'

'The last...' Jenni gasped. 'But that's my bedroom.'

'It was the storeroom in my day,' William told her. 'It looks a whole heap more spartan now.' Then, at her look of horror, he relented. 'Hey, I hauled the bedclothes and the floor rug into the other room before I turned it into a pig residence,' he told her kindly. 'And I remembered your pyjamas.'

'My... My pyjamas...' Jenni could hardly speak. 'I don't believe it. You've put twenty-six pigs in my bedroom!'

'At least twenty-six. I swear I counted more.'

'William Brand, I no longer wish to marry you,' Jenni told him. 'The deal's off.'

'But, hey, they're your pigs in your bedroom,' William told her. Damn him, the man actually looked cheerful. 'Remember, if you don't marry me then they're Ronald's pigs, in Ronald's bedroom.'

There was that, Jenni conceded. It was a comfort—but not much. Jenni thought of the mess she'd be facing in the morning and she shuddered. Ugh!

'There was nowhere else, Jenni,' William said, his voice softening. 'I could hardly tether twenty-six individual pigs. That gate's impossible. The wood's heavy and rotten. Why don't you have a cyclone wire gate put on?'

'I can't afford cyclone wire,' she snapped.

'Well, you can't use my bedroom wall again,' Rachel said firmly. 'I object.'

'I'll find something. I intend to rebuild the pigsty but...'

'But you have the odd other thing on your plate.' William's smile gentled. 'Like welcoming your sisters home. So let's do that now. Come inside. I'll help you clean up after the pigs in the morning—after we rebuild the sty.'

Jenni stared. 'But...you can't...'

'I was born and bred on a farm, Jenni. I can build pigsties.' William's dark eyes twinkled. 'And I can even afford to go into town tomorrow and buy us some cyclone fencing. Just to save Rachel's bedroom wall.'

'You're not spending money on us. And...' Jenni was floundering '...anyway, I thought you were leaving tonight.'

'I was.' He glanced down at his watch. '*Was* is the operative word. My plane takes off about forty minutes from now, from Sydney airport. Three hours' drive away.'

'Oh, I'm sorry!' Jenni's hand flew to her mouth. 'I didn't think... I should have phoned. We shouldn't have waited in town for Rachel—'

'Yes, you should,' Rachel broke in. She'd been standing watching, totally bemused. 'Most definitely you should, 'cos otherwise I wouldn't have met your affianced husband, Jenni, love.' The girl shoved her suitcases on to the ground and took a step forward to take William's hand in a strong, athletic grip. 'Mr Brand, I am very, very happy to meet you,' she said. 'You can't believe how happy. You seem to me to be exactly what Jenni needs.'

'Yeah, well...'

Both Jenni and William suddenly looked uncomfortable.

'Rachel, this is only for twelve months,' Jenni said awkwardly. 'It's not like we're really getting married.'

'But William has to live here. Right?'

'Right. But as our guest, Rach.'

'Oh, sure. Like the pigs.' Rachel grinned. 'Well, all I can say is that this promises to be an interesting twelve months. The man's been here for five hours and already he's paid off the goat's excesses and invited twenty-six pigs to stay. What next?'

'Maybe we could all go in for supper next?' William said diffidently, and this time all the girls stared.

'Supper?' Rachel asked, holding out little hope that she was hearing right. 'You mean... Something to eat?'

'We had dinner in town,' Jenni said, and there was a touch of defiance in her tone. 'And Rachel always eats dinner on the train. So we're not...'

'I mean supper,' William told her, and there was reproof in his voice.

'I guess...'

Oh, help, Jenni thought, floundering. She wasn't used to social settings. Guests and supper. He was expecting to be fed. Of course he was expecting to be fed. She hadn't even organised him any dinner.

This was dreadful. This man had been good to them, even if he had invited twenty-six pigs to stay. Jenni's voice lowered in dismay. 'Oh, help,' she muttered. 'I suppose you're hungry. I'm so sorry. I didn't think. I'm not much into entertaining, you see. I can cook you some eggs.'

'And the bacon's in the back room,' William agreed blandly. 'Hiking around on a hundred and four legs. Jenni, a man could starve. How have you survived for this long without me?'

'On baked beans,' Beth said darkly. 'Jenni thinks she invented baked beans. That and eggs and bananas. I was raised on baked beans and eggs and bananas. I reckon I was twelve years old before she finally found out about our fourth culinary specialty.'

'Which is?'

'Spaghetti.'

'Oh, beaut.' But William was smiling again as Jenni's look of consternation increased. 'No, Jenni, I'm not expecting you to cook for me. Especially I'm not expecting you to cook me baked beans. Heaven forbid. I've cooked myself an omelette, thank you very much, and I ate it an hour ago to celebrate the confinement of the pigs. I raided the garden. There's a nice lot of herbs growing out there.'

'I planted the herbs,' Beth said. 'I like the smell.'

'So do I, but I like the taste better. And for supper I've made us a cake.'

'A cake!' They were all staring in stunned bemusement, as if he'd said the word 'cake' in ancient Greek.

'There's a patch of rhubarb by the back porch that seems to have escaped Herbert's notice,' William told them. 'So we now have a rhubarb and custard cake—oh, by the way, I milked the cows so I haven't used the last of your cream. The cake is waiting for us, right now.'

'You milked the cows?' Jenni said faintly. That was her job. One of her million.

'Yep. They were mooing, telling me very firmly their milkmaid was late. I approve of your choice in cows, by the way. They're very sociable ladies.'

'But…' Jenni stopped, bewildered.

William Brand didn't look like the sort of man who guessed cows needed milking and who then proceeded not only to milk them, but to make a cake with the produce. He looked the sort of man who sat in boardrooms, and told his minions what to do, and escorted beautiful women around town. Oh, and made money...

But Rachel wasn't asking questions. All Jenni's sister was interested in was cake. 'Holy cow!' Rachel picked up a heap of baggage and headed up the verandah, three steps at a time.

'What's keeping us outside, guys?' she called. 'Hurry up before the pigs stage a break-out and get it before we do. Hey, Jenni, this is great. You'd better hurry up and marry the man or I'll marry him myself. He milks cows and he bakes cakes! Well, well. What next?'

William's cake was all very well, but it didn't make her one bit less confused, Jenni thought as they sat around the kitchen table and demolished the last of William's excellent creation. She was getting deeper and deeper into something she didn't understand at all.

'So how come you can cook?' Rachel demanded as Jenni watched in silence. There were times in life when it was useful to have a noisy sister, Jenni decided. There were so many things Jenni wanted to know about William, and she felt as if she couldn't ask any of them, but Rachel knew no such qualms.

'That's how I made my fortune,' William told her.

'Like how?' There wasn't any easy way to avoid questions with Rachel. The first word Rachel had ever learned to say had been 'why?'. One of the reasons she'd wanted to be a doctor was that she was so curious, and she was curious about everything.

'My mum died when I was tiny so I cooked for my dad and me,' William told them. 'When I quit university, cooking was the only thing I was good at. I qualified, went to the US, saved some money, set up my own restaurant—tiny at first—and then started accommodation packages. Gourmet weekends on Long Island. It's gone from there.'

'So you can cook more than rhubarb cakes?' It was still Rachel.

'I can cook most things,' William told them. 'But I don't. Unless in emergencies, like tonight. Like when faced with baked beans. Mostly I have master chefs do my cooking for me.'

Oh, of course. Jenni took another bite of cake and wondered just what it would be like having master chefs doing her cooking for her. She couldn't. She felt as if she was in a daze.

Her sisters were still talking.

'I'd love to cook,' Beth said wistfully. 'It'd be so great. To cook a cake like this…'

'Why don't you?'

Beth glowered. 'Don't be silly. Blind people don't cook.'

'Why not?'

The question hung around them, and Jenni found herself holding her breath. Beth was so touchy. She was just as likely to get up now and storm into her bedroom because of William's insensitivity.

'Because I can't see.' It was such a bitter response it was almost a slap.

Jenni expected William to shut up then, but he did no such thing.

'Yeah, but you can taste. And feel.' He frowned. 'You can't tell me there aren't scales with tactile measures instead of visual ones. You'd need a tactile thermostat on your oven but that should be easy to organise.'

'That's not all.' Beth's bitterness was so deep you could taste it.

'No.' William grew thoughtful, and Jenni could see a sharp intelligence focussing on her sister's problems. 'I guess not. There are things I do by sight, like seeing whether onions are brown or sauce is lumpy.'

'Yeah, so...'

But William wasn't to be stopped. 'But if you used your senses... You could use a cold spoon to taste-test a sauce—it'd cool fast enough for you to feel if it's lumpy. You could learn to time onions, and to smell whether they're right. And you can feel things like meringue for consistency.'

'But I couldn't just *do* it,' Beth said bleakly. 'I'd need a teacher.'

'I'll teach you.'

And then all the girls were staring at him—and William was staring inwardly at himself as he heard what he'd just said.

What had he done here? His plan was to do what he had to do and then leave, with minimal emotional involvement. He was leaving tomorrow for a month, and returning in time for the wedding. Nothing else.

But Beth was looking at him with a face bright with eagerness, and Rachel was smiling her pleasure—and Jenni was looking at him with eyes that couldn't believe what she was hearing.

Jenni had carried her sisters' burdens for ten long years, William thought suddenly. There was only Jenni to help Beth, and Beth deserved to be helped.

'Tomorrow,' Beth said urgently. 'Teach me tomorrow before we go and get Sam. Will you teach me to make a cake like this?'

'William's leaving tomorrow,' Jenni told her.

'I'll get up early.' Beth pushed herself to her feet. 'To learn to make a cake like this, I'll get up at five if I must. Please, William...'

'Not five.' William managed a smile but he was starting to feel almost as confused as Jenni. What was he letting himself in for? 'Nine. Your first cooking lesson is scheduled at nine tomorrow.'

'Then I'll go to bed now.' Beth's face was alight with eagerness. 'And straight to sleep. If you really will help me...'

Rachel pushed herself to her feet as well, regretfully, Jenni thought.

'And I'm home on swat vac,' she said. 'Which means I have exams in a week, so I'm off to hit the books. Jenni, I'll leave you with your soon-to-be-husband.' She bent and kissed her sister on the top of her head.

'And I approve very much,' she whispered. 'Go to it, Jenni.'

And William and Jenni were left alone.

CHAPTER FOUR

OH, HELP...

What did one say, late at night over the kitchen table, to one's affianced husband—when one had only just met one's affianced husband that afternoon?

'Thank...thank you for being nice to Beth,' Jenni managed, but William waved his hand as a disclaimer.

'I'll enjoy teaching her to cook a cake. It'll be a challenge.'

Jenni couldn't think of a single thing more to say.

Finally she pushed herself to her feet. She had to do something here, or she'd go nuts, and she couldn't go to bed. There were pigs in her room!

'I'll walk down and check out the pigsty,' she said. 'If I can get them out of the house and back where they belong...'

'You won't get the gate to work.'

'I've closed that gate every night for the last ten years,' she told him.

'You won't tonight.'

'Want to bet?' she demanded. 'Just because you're a weakling...'

William grinned and rose, his long body towering over her. He filled her tiny kitchen as no one else had ever done.

'Weakling, hey? Okay, Jenni Hartley. Let's go down and see you close this gate.'

Weakling indeed!

She couldn't. No one could.

The child who'd swung open the gate had swung it so wide it had snapped off its rotten hinges. It had always been easy enough to open, falling downhill, but that had been its undoing. With the child pulling it open and then releasing it to swing free, it had fallen so fast the hinge had snapped clean away, the timber railings crumbling as they fell.

So what would she do now? Jenni thought bleakly.

Buy timber to fix it? The railings would be expensive and she needed a new fence post. Jenni did a fast calculation of her bank balance. This and the vet's fees tonight…

Maybe she'd have to use Rachel's wall again. When was Rachel going back to university? And meanwhile…

'Oh, great,' Jenni murmured, acutely aware of William by her side. 'That leaves me…'

'Sharing a bedroom with twenty-six pigs.' William leaned on the fence and grinned at her in the moonlight. 'I wouldn't. I'll just bet they'll snore.' His grin deepened. 'You can share my master bedroom if you like. Master bedrooms are meant to be shared. With mistresses. Or wives.'

'Oh, yeah…' Jenni was so self-conscious that she was finding it hard to breathe. 'In your dreams, William Brand.'

'Well, I am your intended…'

'On paper.' She glowered. 'Get one thing straight right now, William. I am not in the market for a husband apart from a name on a legal piece of paper. You try claiming anything else as a right and I'll tell Ronald he can take the farm. Slime ball or not, it's his.'

William's smile faded. They stood silently by the sty, the tension increasing by the minute.

Of course she was right. He should agree, William thought. That was what he wanted—wasn't it? He should agree that a legal document was all that was required, and then he should take himself back to the house. Put himself to bed and leave in the morning.

But he couldn't. Her harsh affirmation that she didn't want him nettled something deep inside.

This was crazy, William thought. He was at home with women. He didn't have a problem with dating, talking…even sleeping with women. His sex life was entirely satisfactory for his needs, thank you very much. He wanted no involvement, now or in the future. He'd worked that out as a Brand survival technique.

So why was he so tense?

He stared down at Jenni in the moonlight. She looked almost a kid, with her jeans and his oversized shirt and her worn boots, and that absurd braid with wisps escaping.

Suddenly he had an almost overpowering urge to reach out and loosen it completely. To see what her hair looked like, hanging free…

He held back with an effort.

'Why are you so touchy, Jenni?' he asked mildly. 'Can it be you've never had a boyfriend? I find that hard to believe.'

'I don't know why you should.' She glowered. 'I don't have time for boyfriends. Rachel has boyfriends. I don't.'

'Yeah, I'd imagine Rachel having boyfriends.' William grinned. 'Herds of 'em. But you…'

'I told you… Look, William, this subject is out of bounds.'

'Husbands and wives should know all about each other.'

'As long as you're not a bigamist or a serial killer, then I don't need to know any more.'

'But…' The temptation to push this further was almost irresistible. 'You don't want to know me in any other way?'

'No!' It was close to a cry of panic.

'Why not?'

'Look, I just don't…' Jenni backed away, holding up two hands as if to fend off a lunge, and William's brow snapped down in concern.

'Hey, Jenni, let's not go over the top here. I'm not threatening rape of my very own wife.'

'Look, maybe this isn't such a good idea…'

William's frown was still there. 'This isn't making sense, Jenni. You're acting like you're twelve years old and I'm the first male who ever asked if he could kiss you.'

'I'm… I'm…'

And William's eyes widened, and he swore softly into the night. 'You're kidding! You really haven't been kissed?'

'Look, just because everyone's not promiscuous…'

'I'm not promiscuous.'

'Oh, yeah? That's not what the society tabloids say about you.'

'They don't say I'm promiscuous, Jenni.' William shook his head in the dark. 'Dating women isn't necessarily sleeping with them. But this… This is a nonsense. Jenni, somehow we have to convince the world that we have a viable marriage. If the world—or at least the legal fraternity—doesn't believe we have a marriage, for twelve months at least, then Ronald gets his farm. So you'll have to learn not to flinch every time I come near you.'

'I don't flinch.'

'You flinch.'

'Just because you expect every woman to leap right into your arms…'

'I don't, actually,' he said. 'But neither do I expect them to turn frigid and run a mile.'

'Are you saying I'm frigid?'

'Twenty-six and never been kissed… Yes. I definitely call that frigid.'

'Well, I'm not!' Jenni took a deep breath. 'It's just I can't... I can't afford to be distracted. I can't afford the time. I never have...'

'I can see that,' William told her, his voice gentling. 'You've put your whole life into making this farm pay, and you've raised two great sisters. But, Jenni, Beth and Rachel aren't going to be dependent on you all their lives. And when they're gone...'

'Beth will always need me.'

'She may not,' he said softly. 'Beth has brains and spirit and she's aching to be independent. You can't tie her to your apron strings. And then what?'

Jenni's chin tilted and a dangerous sparkle lit behind her eyes.

'Then there's always the pigs.'

'Oh, that's right. You have twenty-six pigs to share your bedroom with. Kinky! You'll turn into a particularly smelly spinster with strange eating habits. And your braid will curl. What a waste!'

'William, this is none of your business.'

'You're my future wife. It's very much my business if my future wife chooses pigs before me. Consider my pride! And surely you're not going to stay here for ever?'

'I don't see why not. I like it here.'

'You've never seen anything else.'

'I like it that way!'

'Well, what about your love life?' he said, ignoring her protest. 'Surely you don't intend to stay single for ever?'

'Why not? I don't need a man.' She grimaced. 'I've seen what marriage does to people and I don't like it. I don't need it.'

'You don't know what you need,' he said sternly. 'My parents had a great marriage until my mother's death. And

sex is great. How can you know if you've never tried? Jenni,
come here.'

'No way.'

'Jenni…' William's dark eyes glinted at her and he
smiled, and the man just had to smile and Jenni's knees
turned to jelly. 'Jenni, this afternoon, I asked you to marry
me and you agreed. Now I find that the woman I intend to
marry has never been kissed. I refuse to let such a state of
affairs continue. It's almost immoral.'

'Immoral!' Jenni somehow found the strength to say the
word. Her knees were wobbling and her foundations were
shaken to the core. 'Immoral! I know who's immoral.'

'I'm not immoral. Jenni, come here and let me kiss you.'

'I don't want to.'

'Liar.'

'I am not—'

Jenni, shut up. Just shut up, put down your bristles and
let yourself be kissed.'

And William took two steps towards her in the moonlight,
took her in his arms—and he kissed her.

Twenty-six and never been kissed…

It wasn't quite true. At sixteen Jenni had been pretty and
vivacious and more than ready for a good time. There had
been boyfriends then, and the first few tentative hand-
holdings and moist kisses in the back of the movie theatre.

None of which Jenni had enjoyed very much.

Then, once, she'd walked in on her father having sex with
his secretary in her parents' bed. Ugh! There was no way
she wanted any part of that.

And then her parents had died. Her world had come crashing down around her, and Jenni's sex life had been put on
indefinite hold. Jenni had watched Rachel's succession of
boyfriends without a pang. She didn't have time for distrac-

tions, and, from what she remembered of boy-girl kisses and
her parents' fighting, she wasn't missing out on anything.

But William… William was something else! William was
enough to make her think again.

His mouth touched hers, and Jenni froze.

First it was just shock—shock that he dared touch her.
Shock at the strangeness of him—the feel of a male mouth
on hers, of strong hands coming around her waist and pulling
her into him.

Shock at the sensations that coursed straight down her
body at his first touch.

And then it was something else. Something other than
shock or physical sensation taking right over. Something
she'd never felt in her life before, and until this moment she
hadn't even known existed.

What was happening to her here?

Jenni stepped back, but William's hands permitted no
freedom. He pulled her close, brooking no opposition. Her
breasts were moulding against his chest and she could feel
the steady beating of his heart beneath hers.

She could feel his strength. She could feel his maleness.

She could feel the pure, unfiltered pleasure of male against
female.

She heard herself give a tiny whimper, but it wasn't dismay. Not that. Confusion?

Maybe.

Or maybe it was desire.

She didn't desire him. She didn't!

But her lips were opening under the strong insistence of
his mouth. She was tasting the maleness of him. Her hands
were circling the broad expanse of his back, daring to hold
him as he was holding her, and suddenly she was kissing
right back.

And this wasn't like any sixteen-year-old fumbling at the back of the movie theatre. This was like...

Like nothing. Like fire. Like a thousand-volt charge zinging back and forth until it seemed as if her body would melt in a pool of molten desire.

And it wasn't just her body. It was her head. Her heart. Her everything!

She groaned with pleasure, her body as alight with desire as his. Oh, William... Her hands pulled his head down to hers, deepening the kiss. Her tongue explored him, tasting him. Wanting him.

Dear heaven, she was out of her depth here. Way out of control.

What on earth was happening? What was she doing?

In a jolt of blind panic she managed to haul herself out of his hold and somehow...somehow stumble back against the remains of the sty wall. There she stood, gazing up at William in the moonlight, her eyes dazed and confused and frightened.

What was happening here? What? She stared up at him in horror and William stared back in the soft moonlight.

And William felt the same massive, earth-moving jolt.

He stared down at Jenni in the dim light—at this slip of half girl, half woman—and he felt his heart twist with something he didn't understand in the least.

This wasn't what was supposed to happen. Love-making...well, you followed certain rules. You kissed and you were kissed in return. And then maybe you ended up in bed or maybe you didn't. But, either way, the woman you kissed didn't stand there looking at you like a frightened doe. As if you were tilting her world on its axis and she didn't understand the new rules...

And neither did you end up feeling like this! As if you

wanted to hold her in your arms and reassure her and tell her... Tell her what?

He didn't know. He didn't have a clue.

Hell! What now? What now, Brand?

He had to get out of here. He had his rules. No involvement.

He had to leave.

But William had promised to teach Beth to bake one cake, and there was the small matter of twenty-six pigs in the back bedroom. He did feel a certain responsibility to help move the pigs out in the morning.

Therefore he couldn't get in his car and go riding off into the sunset right at this minute—much as he thought he should.

'Jenni, maybe we should go inside,' he said, and his voice was none too steady. 'I'm sorry. I shouldn't have done that. I shouldn't have kissed you. This has to stay platonic or we're both in trouble. It'll never work.'

He held out his hand for her to take, and he continued to hold it out.

Jenni stared down at it in the faint light and her mouth gave a bitter little twist. It was almost as if he was offering to help her. Asking her to put her hand in his... To trust him...

She didn't. Not after what had just happened. Her own body was betraying her here, and, if her own body wasn't to be trusted, this man sure as heck wasn't.

'I can walk by myself,' she said with dignity, and William's hand fell away.

He wasn't used to that either. Women knocking back overtures of affection...

Okay. He could play it her way, and maybe her way was best.

'All right. Let's go sort out sleeping arrangements,' he
said softly—and then he turned at the sound of a car being
gunned fast along the gravel of the beach road.

Faster and faster it came, the sound splitting the night—
and then brakes squealed as the car came to a halt right
outside the house.

A flare lit the night. There was a crash—the sound of
breaking glass.

And the flare shot higher into the night and grew.

The house was on fire!

William and Jenni stayed motionless for what must have
been about half a second. It seemed longer. Shock held them
frozen.

But then they moved. Unconsciously William's hand
grabbed Jenni's, and she took it without thinking as they
raced back towards the house at a dead run.

Oh, no…

Jenni was so fearful she couldn't breathe. She couldn't
even think.

The front room was well alight already. The glass pane
in the front door was smashed and there were flames shooting out towards the verandah.

'Go around the back through the back door and get your
sisters out,' William yelled above the roar of the flames. The
fire was still contained in the front room. Jenni would be
safe. 'Fast. Get Rachel and Beth out and then release the
pigs. Move, Jenni…'

And Jenni released William's hand and moved as she'd
never moved in her life.

Which left William wondering what on earth to do…

There was a hose lying beside the front step. William

twisted the tap and the hose buckled as a jet of water spurted out. Great. The water pressure was great!

William shoved the hose through the broken glass of the door, singeing the hairs on his wrist as he did so. Then he let it run, spurting water into the burning room. Even if the end of the hose burned off, it would still run.

Next... Next? Think, man, think...

The fire extinguisher from the car!

Once, years ago, William had seen a car catch fire with appalling consequences—and he'd never travelled without a fire extinguisher since. Even in a hired car like this, he demanded an extinguisher be present.

The hire company had been a bit miffed as they hadn't had a small extinguisher available. Finally the manager had shoved a vast tank into the luggage compartment and shrugged. It was the sort of extinguisher usually reserved for putting out fires the size of, say, the eruption of Mt Helen.

'There you go,' he'd said. 'You can put out a petrol tanker blaze with this one!'

Thank goodness for smart-alec hire car managers, William thought, hauling the extinguisher free. This was just what he needed.

There were other noises starting around him now apart from the crackling roar of the fire. The occupants of the cottages were waking and coming out to find out what was happening. Jenni had obviously released the livestock. Pigs were squealing, and one flew past him in the night.

It was probably the piglet that he'd caught six times tonight already.

There was a woman screaming...

It wasn't someone in the house, though. The screaming was coming from one of the cottages, and there was no fire there.

So where were the girls? Where was Jenni? Surely they should be out now?

William's breath caught in his throat, but then, suddenly, Jenni was beside him, her hands linked tightly in her sisters'.

'Stay right where you are,' William barked. 'Don't move.'

'My books…' Rachel was practically hysterical as Jenni held her back. 'My year's notes.'

'They're not important enough to die for. Stay! I've got the extinguisher. You stay where you are and let me deal with it. Jenni, hold her.' Then, checking that Jenni had both girls under control, he ran forward again up the verandah steps.

The crackling had stopped. The flames were no longer shooting out of the glass in the front door. There was thick black smoke—but no flames.

The hose was still spurting water inwards.

Maybe…

There was a doormat before the door. William lifted it and used it to grab the door handle, turning it cautiously inwards.

A vast tunnel of smoke belched out to greet him.

Coughing, he fell back. He took only seconds to recover and the smoke cleared a little. He held the mat around his face and walked forward, one step inside the house. Through the belching smoke he could barely see, but he could see enough.

There were flames at the side of the room, licking up from the floorboards at the curtains. They were away from the jet of water, and were about to erupt into a mass of flames as the curtains caught. William could just see the orange glow through the smoke. The bulk of shooting flames he'd seen at the start must have come from whatever had been thrown inside. The house itself was only just catching, but the floor rug was on fire and it was spreading.

He lifted the extinguisher and hauled the nozzle high. Foam burst out with such force that he staggered backward.

And there he stayed, spraying everything in sight until the whole place was a sea of foam.

And then water landed on his head.

At first he thought he was imagining it.

No. The water became a jet, spraying down. He tried to look up but could see nothing through smoke and water. The ceiling was ancient plaster. The water was coming straight through.

And then something else did.

Jenni.

There was an almighty crash, the plaster buckled and burst, and Jenni's slight frame crashed down on to the floor below.

She landed right at his feet. On his feet! If he'd been expecting her, maybe he could have caught her. As it was she tumbled down, feet first, and landed in a crumpled heap on the floor.

'Jenni!'

She didn't move. There was one long, heart-stopping moment—a moment so awful William couldn't figure out later how his heart didn't stop completely. A moment when he thought someone might be dead...or so dreadfully injured...

Like Julia...

But then Jenni uncurled from her heap and tried to rise, pushing herself to her feet, coughing and gasping and choking for air. William stooped. His arms came around her. He lifted her and held.

Tight. Close. Not brooking any argument. Letting the mat

he'd been holding across his face fall, so that he too was choking. Holding her to him in a grip of iron.

This wasn't Julia. This was no nightmare revisited. This was Jenni and she was alive.

And then he was staggering outside, leaving the hose squirting and the extinguisher spraying for all they were worth. He no longer cared about them. The fire could burn. All that mattered now was Jenni.

She wasn't Julia. She was alive.

Dear Lord!

They reached no further than two steps out of the house before people were grabbing them and hauling them further from the mess and smoke and the danger. Rachel was sobbing and hugging and scolding the pair of them for being idiots because her books weren't that important, and Beth was feeling every inch of them to make sure they were still in one piece.

'It's okay,' William said as he laid Jenni on the ground and crouched over her. 'At least, I hope to hell it's okay. Jenni...'

'I'm fine.' Jenni's voice was a shaken thread. 'Holy heck... I'm fine. Why didn't you catch me?'

'If you'd told me you were coming I might have.' Good grief, the girl was laughing! 'What in heaven's name were you doing in the roof?'

'The shingles on the roof... They were starting to burn. They're ancient wood. If they'd caught...'

'Sod the shingles.'

'This is my house and I love it,' she said, but she still didn't move a bit, and the laughter gave way to pain.

'Jenni, are you okay?' William's voice was hoarse and thick with smoke.

'I might be.' She still didn't move. 'I think… Did I land on my hip?'

'You landed on my foot,' William told her. 'But I'd say there was hip included there somewhere. Don't tell me it's broken.' He looked up at the sea of faces all around him. Every guest from the cottages was there now. Plus a pig or two. 'Can someone call a doctor?'

'We already did. We called the ambulance,' Florence Haynes volunteered. 'And the fire brigade. And I think my husband also called the police. They should be here any minute.'

They were. Before William could speak again, the night was pierced with sirens. Then there were people everywhere and Jenni was taken away from him as ambulance officers and the local doctor gave her the once-over.

'I think the hips's only badly bruised,' the doctor told her, 'but if it is, then you've been very lucky. I want you to come into hospital so we can make sure. I need an X-ray.'

'I'm not going anywhere.' Jenni's eyes searched behind the doctor's shoulder. 'William…'

William was holding Beth while he watched what was going on, but his eyes had scarcely left Jenni.

'I'm here. Go to hospital, Jenni. I'll take care of things here.'

'I've never been to hospital in my life. I'm not starting now.'

'You've never crashed through burning ceilings before.'

'I have so crashed through ceilings.'

William closed his eyes. 'Then I don't want to know about it. Go to hospital.'

'No.' Jenni shook her head fiercely. 'William, that was Ronald. He started the fire.'

'I know that,' William told her. 'But we'll never be able to prove it. Go…'

'If I go, then I'll never come back.' Jenni's voice was desperate and pleading. 'He'll destroy the farm rather than let me have it. He only wants the land anyway. He'll drive us away.'

'No.'

'But you're leaving tomorrow, and Ronald's so angry. He'll destroy us…' Shock was starting in earnest now. There was terror in Jenni's voice and she heard it herself. And caught it. What was she doing? This was no concern of William's. She caught herself with a massive effort.

'It's… It's no…no matter. But I'm not going to hospital.'

'I told you, Jenni. You must. I'll stay.'

'You can't.'

'Jenni, I'll stay until you're safely settled back here. Until you and your family are safe. I promise.' William knelt down then and touched her smoke-stained face. He could feel the tremors running through her body as the shock set in. 'Jenni, I'll take care of Beth and Rachel and even your twenty-six pigs. And your cows and your chickens and your lunatic goat. I promise. Now go to hospital like the doctor says.'

'But…'

'If the doctor says it's okay, then we'll come and pick you up in the morning,' he told her. 'Me and Beth and Rachel will pick up Sam from the vets and you from the hospital. It's a promise. And nothing will happen while you're away. I swear.'

And he took her hand and gripped it. Hard.

'I promise,' he said.

And Jenni looked up into his grimy, blackened face and

she believed him. And in that instant something slipped away from her. A burden so heavy...

For ten long years she'd born absolute responsibility for this farm and for her sisters. And now... This man was offering to share.

The lifting of the burden, combined with the shock and the pain, made her feel giddy and slightly sick.

'O-okay. I'll go.'

In truth there was little choice. The pain in her hip was searing and she couldn't stop the shakes coursing through her body. But she returned the grip of William's hand with fingers that still held strength. Still held courage.

'Thank you, William,' she whispered. 'Thank you...'

And in that instant William felt the shifting of her burden. He knew what was happening here, and he couldn't avoid it. For most of his adult life, William Brand had sworn he wanted no more emotional entanglements. Ever...

But Jenni's burden... He felt it shifting across on to his broad shoulders, and for the life of him he didn't know whether to be glad—or whether to run a mile.

CHAPTER FIVE

WILLIAM passed a very uncomfortable night.

Rachel and Beth were swept into the holiday cottages and cocooned in motherly concern by the Hayneses and the Pattersons, but William stayed awake.

The fire brigade mopped up and left.

'You did a fine job,' the fire chief told him. 'An old weatherboard place like this... It's a wonder it didn't burn to the ground.'

Before they left they made a discovery. The remains of a bottle lay on the charred floor of the living room, still smelling of petrol.

'It's an amateurish Molotov cocktail,' they said, and the police took it away to use as evidence.

'Not that it'll ever come to that,' a morose police chief told William. 'We know who'll be behind this, but there's no way we'll prove it. He won't have done it himself. He'll have paid a lout to do it for him.'

'You know it, but...'

'Look, we've been after your stepbrother for years,' the police officer told him. 'But the man keeps just one step ahead of us. Oh, we'll interview him—lean on him as much as we can—but I'll guarantee we won't get anywhere near the evidence we need to charge him.'

And then he left, too, promising to return in the morning to go over the events in more detail. Which left William staring at the smoke-stained house and wondering what to do next.

'You can sleep on our living-room floor,' Florence Haynes told him, but William shook his head.

He wouldn't put it past Ronald to come back.

So he stayed where he was, watchful of the damaged house, and when a car cruised by without lights at about three in the morning William was standing in the moonlight, on sentry duty with his garden hose.

It was too dark to make out the car number plates. The car slowed, the occupants saw William and they obviously decided against action. The car took off again into the night, and William knew that Jenni had been right.

If he hadn't stayed on guard, the job would now be finished. One more bottle of petrol...

William had known Ronald Harbertson was vicious, but the enormity of what the man was capable of was sinking in deeper by the minute. And he was supposed to be flying out of here tomorrow. Leaving Jenni to cope...

No one would come back now, he thought. Not tonight. But tomorrow...

Finally William tried to sleep, dozing fitfully under the trees at the front entrance, but half listening for cars. He woke at dawn still feeling exhausted.

And then the day started.

Rachel appeared, bleary-eyed but cheerful. She bounced across to his uncomfortable bed and prodded him with her toe.

'Come on, sleepyhead. Let's see what the damage is before we start work.'

'Work...' William rubbed his eyes and stretched like a big cat. 'There won't be any work done on this place today. I assume the insurance assessors will need to inspect it before we can...' Then he paused, another dreadful thought hitting home. 'That is, if the place is insured.'

'Of course it's insured,' Rachel told him. 'Jenni's not a dope.'

'Then…'

'There are a few other things we need to do apart from repairing burned buildings.' Rachel folded her arms and regarded him with the contempt of the very young for the very old. 'Unless you intend to keep on sleeping.'

'Tell me what they are and then I'll decide.' William was thinking longingly of his king-sized bed in his New York penthouse. Of his vast spa bath. Of a leisurely stroll for some excellent coffee…

'Well, for a start, we have twenty-six pigs to catch,' Rachel told him. 'That'll take hours. And we need to figure out where to put them. There's the milking to do, and then it's change-over day. The Pattersons are leaving in about twenty minutes so we can start then…'

'Start…'

'Jenni usually does the cleaning, but…' Rachel gave him her very nicest child-humouring-adult smile. 'I know you wouldn't want your very own fiancée coming home from hospital to find things still undone. All the cottages have to be scrubbed out and the linen changed. Departure time is ten a.m. and arrival is two p.m. so we only have four hours to do it. We need to sort out the phone, too. See if it's working. Bookings come in all the time, and if the line's out we're in trouble. So…' she prodded him again '…how about getting up, lazybones? Will you help?'

William groaned. 'I'm supposed to be going home to New York today. As fast as my legs will carry me.'

'Not if you want Jenni to keep this farm, you're not,' Rachel told him, with the blithe unconcern of the young dropping their burdens on to their elders. 'Jenni needs you here. If you're going to be her husband, this is where you start. Right now.'

And how was he supposed to respond to that? William winced as he rose to start his day, and he winced because Rachel was right.

She was right in more ways than one, William thought grimly. Jenni didn't need a husband at the end of the month. She needed a husband right now.

It was three in the afternoon before William appeared at the hospital to collect Jenni. She'd dressed, reusing the filthy clothes she'd worn the night before, and was limping back and forth across the ward while she waited. When William walked in, bearing a straggly bunch of scorched daisies, she practically fell on his chest in relief.

What was it about this man? She'd known him for twenty-four hours and she was so pleased to see him she felt like weeping.

It was reaction, she told herself fiercely. Reaction and worry.

'William, where have you been?' she demanded, trying really hard not to throw her arms around his neck. 'I've been trying and trying to contact you. Do you know the phone's out, and I couldn't afford a taxi to take me all the way out to the farm? Where are Beth and Rachel? How's Sam? And why the heck are you bringing me burned daisies?'

She paused for breath right before him, though she managed to avoid the neck-hugging, and William grinned. She really was very young. Every single emotion she was feeling was written right across her face. There was no city sophistication about this girl.

He guessed anxiety was her foremost feeling, and it was growing by the minute as she waited for his answers. He took her shoulders and gently propelled her back on to the bed. 'Whoa. One question at a time, Jenni.'

'Take me home.' The feel of his hands on her shoulders

was doing strange things to her. Her voice came out a squeak.

'Not until I've talked to your doctor.' And then, as she opened her mouth with yet more protests, he placed a hand on her lips and effectively silenced her.

'Wait,' he told her. 'Here are your answers. No, the phone's not working, but repairmen are at the farm as we speak. Two, we knew you didn't have the money for a taxi, but we decided you needed to rest. We telephoned earlier. The sister in charge said you were asleep, so we left you here.'

'But—'

The hand clamped back down. 'Shut up, Jenni, dearest,' William said, and his smile deepened. 'Three, Rachel's in the Pattersons' Kookaburra Cottage catching up on study before this evening's party. I know the Brownlows were supposed to be arriving this morning, but we rang them and cancelled their booking.'

'William—' Jenni was struggling for breath.

'I haven't finished yet. I'm up to four and five. Sam is fine. He's limping a little but not as much as you. The vet delivered him home this morning. The vet heard about the fire. The whole town has heard of the fire and everyone wants to help. Beth and Sam are now staying with the Haynes family. They're busy planning the party.'

'Beth!' Stunned, Jenni let herself be propelled back on to the softness of the bed and she sat down with a thump. 'William, what do you mean, she's in with the Hayneses? She's too shy! She'd never voluntarily go anywhere.'

'Florence Haynes wouldn't take no for an answer, and, seeing as there's so much to do, Beth didn't mind at all. I left her blowing up balloons, with Sam supervising.'

'But… Party? What party?' Jenni's mind was in overdrive. 'And if the Hayneses have Beth…I won't be able to charge them full rates. And what of the Brownlows? You can't cancel on the morning of their arrival. They'll sue.'

'They're happy with their alternative accommodation.'

There was a moment's pregnant silence while Jenni thought this through. 'What alternative accommodation?' she asked at last, in a voice of deep foreboding, and William smiled.

'It's a place just north of Bateman's Bay that Rachel suggested. It's called Lagoona Resort. I'm paying the difference between the costs of the resort and what they would have paid for Kookaburra.'

'But...' Jenni gasped. 'Lagoona Resort... It's fabulous. Five stars. All meals are provided and it costs a bomb.'

'That's why the Brownlows are happy with the deal.'

'I'll bet they are.' Jenni took two deep breaths and then another, but still she felt panic threatening to overwhelm her. 'William, I can't afford this. No way. It's crazy. Just because you have heaps of money, it doesn't mean we do. We have to eat, and...'

'But, Jenni, I have one piece of really good news,' William said, in a voice that declared all Jenni's troubles were over. 'In view of the fire, Mrs Pilkington's willing to forget about Herbert and the beach coat. She gave me our money back.'

'Gee, that's great.' Jenni was practically speechless with fury. 'Of all the arrogant, overbearing, too-rich-for-your-own-good stupid statements... One beach coat compared to two weeks' holiday rental!'

'It *is* great, isn't it?' William sat down on the bed beside her and took her hand in his. He ignored her angry gasp and the way she pulled back on her hand—he knew she really didn't want him to let go—and he kept right on talking. 'Now, while you're still in a good mood—'

'I'm not in a good mood,' she yelled. 'Let go of my hand.'

'Hush,' said the ward sister from the door. She'd been listening in on every word and was thoroughly enjoying herself.

She was ignored. Both parties were deep in battle.

'While you're still in a good mood,' William repeated firmly, 'let me tell you what else we've organised.'

'"We"? I don't want *you* to organise anything. Who's "we"?'

'Me and Rachel and Beth and the Hayneses and the Pattersons and the vet and Mr Clarins and everyone else who could put an oar in this morning. So shut up and listen.'

'William, I want to go home. Now! You have no right—'

'When you've listened. First, we've loaned the cows to your next-door neighbour for a few days. He'll milk them with his herd and supply you with milk. Then you'll be delighted to learn we've made a great new run for the pigs. I know when your house burns down that housing pigs is hardly a priority, but while the guests were sympathetic it seemed a waste not to put them to work.'

'You put the guests to work!'

'Yep. The Pattersons and Pilkingtons even delayed their departure so they could help. I had two chaps from the fencing company come out and rebuild the sty, so we had somewhere to put them.'

'But you know I can't afford fencing.' Jenni's voice was practically a wail.

'William, are you crazy?'

'But I can.' The dratted man seemed totally oblivious to her distress. 'No sweat. We've moved everything that's not smoke-stained into Kookaburra Cottage. That's where we'll base ourselves until we clean the house. Beth and Sam will stay with the Hayneses. Then you and Rachel can have one room in Kookaburra, and I'll have the other.'

'I won't…'

'You won't want to share with Rachel?' William appeared to brighten. He looked down at his scorched daisies with affection and his voice filled with gentle laughter. 'Rachel said you wouldn't. She says she talks in her sleep. Hey, was it worth picking these daisies, then? Mrs Haynes said I should bring you flowers but I wasn't sure. But now... Of course you can share with me rather than bunk in with Rachel. After all, Rachel would study much better if she had her own room!'

Jenni gasped. She was all at sea here, and she wasn't enjoying herself one bit. William was teasing—surely he was!—but she wasn't feeling the least bit like laughter.

'William, no,' she managed, and she had enough anger to make her voice work. Autocratic males! Who did he think he was? 'I'm not staying in Kookaburra. I need to rent it out. We need the money. I'll stay in the house. I don't mind a bit of smoke and water.'

'You wouldn't want to know about the house,' William told her darkly. 'Not yet. It's a quagmire of wet soot. I'm good, but I'm not so good I can get houses rebuilt by dusk.'

'But...' Jenni's voice faltered, and now there was real fear on her face. Her anger was supplanted by terror. 'Rebuilt? What do you mean? William, the house didn't look so bad.'

'It's not,' he told her quickly, laughter fading completely in the face of her fear. 'The front room is damaged, but that won't cost too much. I'll move builders in as soon as the insurance assessors move out. But there's smoke and water damage in the other rooms. I have to tell you, Jenni, that Beth and Rachel's belongings are pretty much okay, but yours...'

'They're not burned!'

'No, they're not burned, but...'

'The pigs.' Jenni stared at him in horror. 'Of course. The pigs...'

'The pigs didn't get into your wardrobe or drawers,' he told her, and his magnetic grin flashed out again. 'More's the pity. But the hole you made let the smoke into the ceiling cavity. The only manhole downward was in your room. The smoke's gone through everything.'

'But…'

'And then the water… Did you know you dropped the hose when you fell? It sprayed into your room and the combination of smoke and water… Plus pig smell.' He shook his head solemnly. 'Not a good mix, Jenni.'

'But…' Jenni shook her head, trying to clear the fog. 'It doesn't matter. My clothes are old. If it's only smoke and pig smell…'

'You know, that's what Rachel told me,' William said. 'And Rachel said what a pity they hadn't been burned. So you won't get too sad that Rach and I decided they needed replacing. And Beth concurred. So we've decided—'

'We!'

Jenni was practically speechless. To have someone else make decisions…

It was *Jenni* who made the decisions. It was *always* Jenni who made the decisions. To have someone else dictate was taking her breath away.

'The parents of one of Beth's school friends run a fashion house at Bateman's Bay,' William told her, seemingly ignorant of her speechless astonishment. 'Beth phoned them—'

'You haven't got a phone.' Jenni was fighting for facts here. Fighting for anything.

'Beth called them on my mobile phone,' William explained patiently. 'And they're expecting us. We decided you can't face fire and disaster and insurance assessors in grimed and smoke-stained jeans. And especially you can't face the party we've planned.' His twinkling smile reached

out and encompassed her. All of her, from braid to boots.
'Not that you don't look great!'

Jenni flushed again, and kept right on flushing. Oh, heck!
She didn't feel great. She felt grimy and bruised and battered
and…and out of control. She felt perfectly dreadful and she
was feeling worse by the minute. And…*what party*?

'But…are you sure you should come home yet?' William
asked, watching the emotions wash over her face. 'I'll ask
the doctor. We can put things off by twenty-four hours if
we must.'

'The doctor says I can,' Jenni said desperately. 'He
says—'

'The doctor says she has the mother and father of a bruise
on her upper leg but she's been lucky to escape a break.' It
was the doctor himself, elderly and dapper and walking
briskly into the ward. He smiled at both of them, and shook
William's hand as he rose to greet him.

'Well, well. William Brand.' The doctor beamed. 'I knew
your father and I remember you when you were knee-high
to a grasshopper. And Henry Clarins tells me you're marrying our Jenni this evening. Excellent. Couldn't be better.
My wife and I will be there. With the general invitation
you've issued, it's my guess the whole town will be present.
I'm not the one to be standing in your way. I'm letting her
go, but on the condition that she rests when she feels like
it. Look after her, boy. You can organise that?'

'Yes, sir.'

'What the…? No, he can't,' Jenni burst out, staring up at
both men, appalled. 'Look, this is a mistake. We're not marrying this evening. We're not being married for a month. I
can't—'

'Yes, you can, Jenni.' William smiled. 'We need to do a
bit of clothes-buying first, though, Doctor…'

'Wouldn't hurt in the least. Buy her something pretty,' the

doctor growled. 'She deserves it.' And then he paused. 'I take it the farm's safe enough from Harbertson while you organise things? The whole district knows what he's trying to do.'

'I've employed security guards.'

'You've what?' It was all Jenni could do not to yell. 'With whose money?'

'With our money, sweetheart.' Ignoring the venom she was firing at him, William helped her off the bed and stood with his arm around her waist. 'You're forgetting our vows, my love. As of our wedding day—as of this day—what's yours is mine and what's mine is yours.'

'We're not married yet,' she said through gritted teeth, but William grinned and swept her straight up to cradle her in his arms. He held her tightly against him, claiming her as his own.

'Nope. You're not. More's the shame. Not for a whole four hours, you're not my bride, but I'm starting to think I can't wait. Do you know you look really, really cute when you're angry? Now, though… If you'll excuse us, Doctor, my future wife and I need to go shopping. And then we have a wedding to attend. Ours.'

Crazy.

This was just crazy.

Jenni sat in the passenger seat of William's sports car and fumed while William signed discharge papers and said goodbye to the nurses and generally acted as if he were the husband of someone who was a little bit simple. And the nurses lapped him up. Two of them came out to say goodbye, and it was William their eyes rested on as the car left the hospital car park—not Jenni.

'And now,' Jenni said as they turned on to the highway

leading north to Bateman's Bay. 'Now, do you mind telling me what's going on? What *on earth* is going on?'

'I'm defending my family and our farm from Ronald,' William said mildly. 'Isn't that what any red-blooded husband should do?'

'Defending...' Jenni shook her head. 'William, stop.'

'Stop?'

'Stop this car and tell me what's going on,' she demanded. 'Before I open the car door and jump. I swear I will.'

'You'll end up back in hospital.'

'Then maybe it's a sane alternative to staying in the car with you. William, *stop*!'

So William stopped. He pulled into a parking bay looking over the town and out to sea. There were yachts sailing on the bay. The sun was glinting on the water. Betangera looked serene and lovely.

Serene... The total opposite to how Jenni was feeling.

'Tell me...'

'Tell you what?'

'Well, for a start...' Jenni took a deep breath '...am I still in last night's bad dream, or did the doctor infer we were marrying today?'

'You're not dreaming. It's the only way, Jenni,' William said apologetically. 'I've looked at it from every angle. We need to be married now.'

'But...why?'

'I spent a couple of hours with your lawyer, Henry Clarins, this morning,' William told her. 'He took legal advice from a couple of mates in Sydney. Once we're married, the only way Ronald can upset the legacy is by proving we're not living together as husband and wife. Disasters can't give him the farm.'

'I don't understand...'

'If you or I died now, before we're married, then Harbertson inherits,' William said grimly. 'I'm sure if you'd died last night then he'd have been delighted. But once we're married Ronald won't inherit, no matter what happens. The legal advice is that, if we were living as husband and wife at the time of our death, then Beth or Rachel would inherit, or we could bequeath it to a cats' home if we like. Legally we'd still be trying to fulfil the conditions of the will, so death wouldn't void the legacy. Ronald won't get it.'

'But…'

'But until we're married we're vulnerable.' William's smile was now a million miles away. His grim voice told Jenni he was in deadly earnest. 'Jenni, I spent a lot of last night thinking things through. Yesterday Ronald showed us a taste of what he's capable of. The police say he's capable of more.'

'He won't hurt us.'

'He already has.' William paused and his mouth tightened into an unyielding line. 'If we hadn't been awake last night then someone may well have died in the fire. And, Jenni, if something happened to Beth… If there was a blackmail attempt, with Ronald threatening things like…well, if you marry then Beth will die—something like that—then would you marry?'

'Of course not,' Jenni said. 'But…'

'You're not only vulnerable through you,' William told her. 'You're vulnerable through Beth and Rachel and Sam and your farm. Anything could happen and Harbertson has a month to plan that ''anything''. The police chief thinks he will. The farm could be sold to developers for a tidy sum and the man's desperate. The police say he's up to his ears in debt and some heavyweight criminals are after him. Deservedly. But he's not getting the farm to pay for his criminal activities. This way…'

'Yeah, this way…' Jenni took a deep breath. 'This way,

I don't understand even more. How can we marry today?
We need a month's notice.'

'A Clerk of Courts can give us special dispensation,'
William told her. 'Henry Clarins told me this morning. He'd
been thinking things through, and when he heard about the
fire he made a special trip out to the farm to tell me. If we
can prove we've known each other for ever and the intention
to marry is solid and sensible, then we can get a dispensation. They don't like doing it, but in special cases they'll
grant it. Henry Clarins' friend is the local Clerk of Courts.
Henry's already talked to him and told him to expect us for
an interview.'

'But...'

William glanced at his watch. 'Jenni, he's expecting us at
five. So we go there straight after finding you something
decent to wear. We'll get our dispensation, and then the
marriage celebrant's meeting us at the farm at seven. To
marry us.'

'That's the party!' Jenni felt as if all the breath had been
knocked out of her lungs. Things were becoming clear. Not
sane, but clear. 'William, that's what you meant when you
said about the party!'

'That's the one.' William's engaging grin lit his face
again, humour flooding back. 'You should have seen
Florence Haynes's face when I suggested she organise a
wedding. She was aching to help, but she didn't expect a
request like this. But I talked it through with Beth and
Rachel. Also with the police chief and the vet and the fencing blokes and the telephone technicians and everyone else
who was at our farm this morning. They all thought it was
a wonderful idea. They're organising things from their end
now. The local caterers are moving in fast. There's a jazz
band on its way. The marriage celebrant is booked. All we

need to do is get our dispensation and buy one wedding dress. And two rings.'

'William…'

'Jenni?'

He was still smiling, that dangerous, endearing, calculating smile that could have won him the world. That had Jenni's heart standing still in her chest.

His smile made her so fearful that she wanted to run a mile—and for the life of her she didn't know what she was fearful of.

'William, this is crazy. I—I don't even know whether I want to be married,' she stammered.

'Of course you do. We talked it over.'

'Yeah, and I was going to have a month to think it through properly before we committed ourselves to the idea,' Jenni wailed. 'A month.'

'And now you have about four hours.' William turned then within the cramped confines of the little car, and he took her hands in his. Two strong, capable hands. Two hands to still the panic.

'Jenni, we can do this,' he said softly. 'We must. I won't have Harbertson hurting you, or hurting Rachel or Beth or Sam. I want us legally married, Jenni, before any more damage is done.'

'But you don't want to be married.'

William's mouth tightened again then, and he sighed. He looked down at Jenni for a very long time and when he spoke again there was grimness in his voice.

'No, Jenni, I don't,' he admitted. 'I used to think the last thing I ever wanted was to be married. But then I thought the last thing I wanted was for Harbertson to inherit my father's farm. And now I think the last thing I want is for Harbertson to hurt you or Beth or Rachel.

'So we'll marry, Jenni,' he said softly. 'We'll marry now.

It's the only way I can keep you safe. We'll marry properly, with all the town to witness it. And if Harbertson arrives to witness the ceremony as well, then we'll even welcome him. We'll marry now, Jenni, and we'll think of everything else later.'

CHAPTER SIX

THERE was nothing more to be said. There were no more arguments to be mounted. The decision had been made. Now all they had to do was carry it through.

First, buy the clothes.

Buying clothes was more weird than being married, Jenni decided. Beth's friend's parents owned one of the most exclusive boutiques on the coast. Whatever Beth had said to prepare them, it had certainly worked. Sally and Harry Parkes were waiting for them in the shop, with tea and sandwiches and smiles of welcome—and a whole shop full of clothes to choose from.

One of their daughters was blind. Beth had been a real friend to Lisa, and Lisa's parents were now eager to do anything they could to help.

But Jenni hadn't been out of a pair of jeans since she was sixteen.

'Do I really need a wedding dress?' she demanded, but William wasn't in the mood to brook arguments.

'Of course you need a wedding dress. This has to be a proper wedding, Jenni. It's a declaration to the entire district that we're married. How about this?' He held up one of the gowns Sally had produced—a magnificent confection of diamanté tulle and lace.

'I'd feel silly,' Jenni retorted, fighting to get her breath back. 'Like the doll on the top of the wedding cake.'

'Hey, I hope Florence and the caterers have thought of a wedding cake,' William said, and frowned. 'Sally, make her try it on while I phone.'

'You really are getting married tonight?' Sally demanded and William nodded, already dialling.

'Yep. Would you like to come?' he asked. 'You're very welcome. All the district is welcome. Bring your daughters so Beth has some company.'

'Goodness!' Sally sighed in delight, romantic stars lighting in her maternal eyes. 'Oh, if it's really tonight…' She took a deep breath and looked Jenni over from head to toe. Then she looked at her husband-cum-business-partner, and she came to a decision. 'Harry, I don't think these gowns are right for Jenni.'

'What's wrong with these gowns?' Harry demanded, dollar signs in his eyes, but his wife wasn't to be distracted.

'If Jenni agrees, then she's borrowing mine,' Sally pronounced. 'The dress I wore thirty years ago. Oh, Jenni, both my daughters are too tall, but it's just the most beautiful gown, and it'd fit you to perfection. Wait until you see it.'

'But—'

'Not a word,' Sally declared. 'Just try it.'

It certainly did fit.

While Harry and William waited outside the changing rooms, Sally worked her magic.

Sally's bridal gown was made with aged silk. The silk had mellowed to a rich, deep cream over the years. There were hand-embroidered, tiny, deep gold roses all over the wondrous, billowing skirt. The bodice was soft and clinging and simple—a low bodice with off-the-shoulder slivers of silk just holding it up.

Not that it needed to be held up. The dress fitted Jenni as if it were made for her. As Sally fastened the last silk-covered button, Jenni stared at her reflection in open-mouthed astonishment.

'And now the hair,' Sally said in satisfaction, and before Jenni could stop her she'd undone Jenni's braid and let it fall free. Jenni's rich black curls tumbled free in a riotous mass around her shoulders.

Good grief! It was as if there were two Jennis. The Jenni before and the Jenni after.

The jean-clad work-horse Jenni. And this... This vision of ethereal beauty.

In this dress, Jenni could forget she had calloused fingers, work-worn hands and a damaged hip. This was a Jenni she'd never met before. Her green eyes were huge, and her dark hair formed a halo effect around her pale face.

'So come out and show us,' William demanded, but Sally was whisking herself between Jenni and the door.

'You'll do no such thing, Jenni Hartley,' she declared. 'It's enough that William's already seen you on your wedding day, but as for seeing you in your dress... No way! So what do you think, Jenni? Will you wear my dress?'

Sally's eyes were suddenly anxious, and Jenni knew that wearing this exquisite dress would give this lady real pleasure.

And Jenni really was going to get married! This wasn't some crazy dream. She felt like pinching herself to make herself wake, but, no matter how hard she pinched, the dream was still there. It was real, and she must make an effort.

'Sally, I'd love to wear this.' Jenni smoothed the rich silk fabric with reverence. 'I've never dreamed of wearing such a dress. Please. But... I'll only wear it if you come to...come to our wedding.'

There. She'd said it.

Our wedding.

She was marrying William. *She was marrying William in about three hours' time!*

'Wild horses wouldn't keep me away,' Sally declared. 'I've just decided that I'm doing your hair and make-up. Oh, and I'll bet you don't have any cosmetics. What a good thing I have two teenage daughters. Between them they have every cosmetic known to womankind and, if they're invited too, they'll be only too delighted to let you use them.'

'Hey, what about the wedding dress?' Harry demanded from outside the cubicle. 'I can't believe you're doing this, Sally. Lending the girl yours when we could be selling her a new one from stock.'

'You'll be doing heaps more selling,' William growled. He was starting to feel just a bit miffed, standing outside the changing rooms. He *really* wanted to see. 'Sally, there's no way Jenni's walking out the door in the clothes she wore in. They're destined for another fire. So I want you to buy a wardrobe of clothes, Jenni. A wardrobe that befits my bride.'

'A wardrobe!' Jenni gasped and turned to face the door, but Sally was still holding it firmly shut between them. 'Look, William, maybe I'll buy a new pair of jeans, but that's all.'

'We don't stock jeans,' Harry told her, sticking in his oar. 'And don't you dare lend the girl yours, Sally.' Then he brightened. 'But we have lovely trousers. And the most beautiful day dresses.'

'You hear that, Jenni? Harry doesn't stock jeans and Sally isn't allowed to lend you any. But they have all sorts of other clothes.' Jenni could hear laughter resurfacing in William's voice and she gritted her teeth.

'Then I'll go someplace else.'

'You'll have to hike there in your wedding dress, because I'm serious, Jenni. You're not wearing those awful clothes out of here. Not if I have to tie you down and carry you stark naked. So choose some new ones.'

'But I don't want new clothes,' Jenni wailed.

'Yes, you do,' William said kindly. 'Jenni, until yesterday you didn't even know you wanted to be married. And now…here you are, all togged up with bridal finery and getting married in three hours' time. Which reminds me, we still have to meet the Clerk of Courts. So hurry up, there's a love. Choose something great!'

'I can't afford…'

'Jenni, I am not marrying a grub,' William said direfully. 'So choose. Do you want to be married or not? The clothes are on me. You know I can afford them and I'll enjoy paying for 'em. So shut up, Jenni, and choose. Sally, Harry, let's get this girl dressed as befits her future status. Wife to me.'

And Jenni was left with nothing more to say. There were no arguments left.

It was a subdued Jenni who walked out of the shop nearly an hour later. She was wearing a simple pastel dress in soft lime-green, and matching sandals. It was smart but not exceptional. It wasn't the sort of dress that would normally turn heads in Bateman's Bay, but it showed Jenni's lovely figure to advantage, and she was pretty enough to draw attention.

Jenni was unaware of heads turning to watch her pass. She had enough to think about. She felt so… So strange. Weird. She hadn't worn a dress in ten years. She felt…

'It's like I'm wearing another skin,' she said, feeling the sensation of the soft cotton against her bare legs. They'd left the rest of her chosen clothes to be packed and delivered by Harry and Sally. Sally was bringing the bridal gown out to Betangera in time for the wedding, and Jenni's new wardrobe would be delivered then.

'You look great.' William caught her hands and pulled her around to face him. Passers-by detoured around them but William seemed unconcerned that they were blocking the pavement. His eyes rested on Jenni. 'Great,' he repeated softly. 'Now, if you'd let your hair free…'

'No way.' Jenni had rebraided it. With her hair free, she felt so strange she was practically not Jenni.

'You'll let it out this evening, though? When we marry?'

'I don't see the point,' Jenni said, but her voice was suddenly breathless. William's eyes, resting on hers, made her feel even weirder than her new clothes did.

'Will you do it because I'm asking you too?'

Another deep breath. The world was shifting from side to side, so fast she must surely fall off. 'I don't... I don't understand.'

'Just do it, Jenni,' William said gently, and he didn't understand what he was doing himself. It should make no difference at all—what she wore to their wedding. This was a business arrangement. Nothing more.

Wasn't it?

The Clerk of Courts didn't think this was a business arrangement—nor could he be allowed to think it.

'He has to believe this marriage has been intended between us for years,' William told Jenni as they waited in his outer office. 'Henry's told him we've been fond of each other since we were kids.'

'Do you remember me as a kid?' Jenni demanded, and William nodded definitely.

'Absolutely. I remember you at the final Christmas I spent at home. You ate the last lamington and I didn't get any.'

'Now that's a great basis for a marriage!' Jenni chuckled, and it was a smiling pair holding hands and looking almost in love that the elderly Clerk of Courts found when he opened the door to usher them in.

His questions were probing and Jenni found them very uncomfortable. She didn't do the talking. She left that to William. He was in charge here.

That in itself was unsettling. She wasn't accustomed to

anyone else being in charge, and she wasn't sure that she liked it one bit—but William was sweeping all before him.

'Jenni and I have always known we'd marry.' He smiled down at Jenni and the look he gave her almost had her believing in his unswerving devotion. 'But... I guess you've heard of what my stepbrother is trying to do? Henry Clarins has told you? That's pushed things forward. We need to marry at once. Once Jenni's my wife, then she's safe.' And he pulled her in close to him, protectively, and Jenni was forced to let her body mould into his.

She had to play the game too. Now, if she could manage an adoring smile up at her betrothed...

She tried. William looked down into her eyes in matching devotion, and Jenni felt like choking in laughter. This was *so* soppy...

'But if it wasn't for Mrs Brand's will... If it wasn't for Harbertson's threats...would you still marry?' the Clerk probed, and William held Jenni closer.

'Maybe it would have taken a bit longer for us to get around to it,' he admitted, still smiling down at his bride. 'I've been overseas, sir, making my fortune, and I've put my emotional life on the back boiler. Jenni's always known that I'm here for her but...well, one gets caught up with business. But now...I love her, and it's time I settled down. I'll stay at Betangera and I'll take care of my wife and that's a promise. I'm not going into this lightly, sir. Jenni's the most amazing woman I've ever met. She's wonderful. It will be an honour to call her my wife.'

And the glint of humour had slipped from William's eyes. His voice was deathly serious. Jenni stared up at him and she felt her own laughter slipping away.

This wasn't crazy. This was...

Real?

No. Impossible.

But now the Clerk was turning to her. 'And you, Miss Hartley? Do you love this man?'

'I...I guess I do.' They were impossible words to say, but it was impossible to say anything else. Not when William's eyes were resting on hers. She'd wondered if she could lie, but now... 'Yes, sir.'

It slipped out like the most natural thing in the world. It didn't seem a lie at all.

'And can you see yourself married to him fifty years from now?'

That was an unexpected question. But William's eyes were still on hers, warm and caring, and his arm was holding her against him. She could feel the steady beating of his heart against hers.

Fifty years...

'If you're still around...' she told the Clerk steadily, and her own arms came around William. And held. 'If you're still around, sir, we'll invite you to the party we'll hold. For our golden wedding.'

'And if I'm still up to dancing when I'm a hundred and sixteen then it would give me great pleasure to come.' The Clerk of Courts beamed and reached over his desk for the necessary documents. 'You make a lovely couple, if I may say so, and I'm not the man to stand in the way of such a determined young pair. I wish you all the very best.'

After that, all they had to do was to get married.

They returned to the farm, and both were silent as they drove. It was as if both needed some time out to let things settle.

Or...it was as if they were afraid to speak. The vows they'd made had been false—hadn't they?

What was happening here didn't make sense.

So silence it was until they pulled up in front of the farm-house, and Jenni then practically gaped. Good grief!

The place had been transformed. Taken over. Overwhelmed by wedding!

There was a vast white marquee in front of the farmhouse, completely blocking the sight of the fire-damaged house. There were balloons and streamers and garlands of every flower known to man strung from tree to tree. There were people—a veritable army of people. Florists groaning under flower garlands and bouquets and flower bowls. Caterers with boxes of cutlery and crockery and plates and plates of food. There were two vast spit barbecues, already roasting…

And every cottage was decorated. Jenni stared out in stunned amazement, recognising guests who came year after year to holiday here but had only been booked in this after-noon. Instead of starting their holidays with a relaxing swim or sleep on the beach, every guest was starting his or her holiday by making preparations for a wedding!

So many people…

And then Rachel and Beth were racing across the yard to tug Jenni's car door open. Sam was back in harness. He was stiff-legged but he seemed almost as excited as his owner. Bother his sore leg. He had work to do!

'Here's the bride,' the girls squealed. 'The bride! Oh, Jenni, Sally's brought out the dress and it's fabulous and she says the minute you arrive—*the minute!*—we're to bring you straight to her in Kookaburra because it'll take her an hour to do your hair and make-up. The photographer will be here in less than that.'

'The photographer…' Jenni stared, bewildered, as Beth and Rachel hauled her from the car. 'The…'

'We've got everything,' Beth said jubilantly. 'William's done most but we've done heaps and Henry Clarins brought out the whole Rotary Club and their wives. What they've done... We couldn't have put this on better if we'd had a year to organise it instead of a day. Sally even brought out bridesmaid's dresses for us and they're lovely. This is a real wedding, Jenni.' She hugged her sister hard, and Sam joined in with a lick or two. 'Come on, Jenni. This is the best...'

Who knew?

Who knew whether it was the best? Apart from the simple civil ceremony between William's father and the horrible Martha, Jenni had never been to a wedding in her life, so she had nothing to compare it to. But as far as lavish went.... As far as fun went... As far as noise and laughter and music and happiness went, then this wedding couldn't be surpassed.

Apart from Ronald—a fleeting shadow in the bushland who came and stared morosely at the marrying couple and then disappeared as silently as he'd come—there wasn't a person here who wasn't determined to enjoy themselves. And when the marriage celebrant asked William to kiss the bride and he lifted the veil to kiss her tenderly on the lips there wasn't a dry eye in the house.

It was the wedding to end all weddings.

It was only Jenni who felt the world was spinning crazily without her and she was no longer on board. She simply had no idea of what was happening.

They danced all night, with Jenni whirling from one partner to another. Her damaged hip was forgotten. She could no longer feel it.

She could no longer feel anything.

Everyone danced until the wee small hours, and then, as the hundreds of guests finally started to depart, William pulled his bride into his arms and held her close.

'Come on, Jenni,' he said softly. 'It's time for the bride and groom to start their married life.'

'So…where do we go?' she faltered, and he smiled.

'Back to Kookaburra. This is the beginning of where we start pretending. We pull down the blinds and let the whole world imagine our bridal night.'

'N—no.'

Jenni bit her lip. This was a dream. It was a strange surrealistic dream, but it was a lovely dream, and she wasn't about to leave it yet. She didn't want to walk into Kookaburra, close the door and go calmly to separate bedrooms.

Not yet.

'Then…where?' William was looking down at his bride with tenderness. Dear heaven, she was lovely. Her dress was just beautiful, and it clung and shimmered and hinted at her lovely body beneath. Someone had persuaded her to let her hair free. It tumbled around her shoulders in a mass of rich black curls. Her face was pale and her eyes too big for her face, but there was just a tinge of colour about her cheeks.

It was as if she was embarrassed. No. As if she was…

In love?

Hey, leave that, Brand, he told himself. It must be the first. As if she was embarrassed.

'I want to go to the beach,' Jenni said softly. 'There's no way I can sleep yet. I need a walk. Will you come?'

It shouldn't matter if he did or not, she thought, but in reality it did. It mattered very much.

There were still guests milling around, making their way slowly to their cars, unwilling for this lovely night to end. William stared around at them, and then he looked down at his bride.

'Your leg must be hurting,' he said softly.

'I've forgotten I have a leg.'

'Then it's numb. Same thing. I'll take you for a walk, but we'll do it my way.'

And before she could utter a squeak of protest William had lifted her up into his arms. They stood, William dark-suited and handsome—impossibly handsome, Jenni thought—and Jenni, breathless and beautiful with her exquisite gown falling in soft folds around her and her curls tumbling around her face.

They were a sight to take the breath away.

'Goodnight, all,' William called to the departing guests. 'Goodnight. This is where we leave you. It's after midnight. My mermaid's losing the use of her legs so I'm taking her back to the ocean.'

And as the crowd parted around them, laughing and cheering and wishing them well, William carried his lady down to the sea.

They didn't stop until they'd rounded the headland and were out of sight of everyone. The moon was still up, a crescent of silver-gold low in the sky, but bright enough to show William the way.

Not that he needed to be shown. The beach was wide and clean and lovely. The waves were silver-white tongues of foam, roving over the blackness of the ocean. The air was still and warm, with the promise of a hot day to come.

The heat would wait, though.

The day would wait.

Once they'd rounded the headland, Jenni struggled in his arms. 'Let me down. Please, William, I need to walk.'

'You'll hurt your leg.'

'Not me. Don't you know?' she retorted as he set her down on the sand. 'I'm as tough as old boots.'

'Not so tough, Jenni.' He touched her face, lifting a wispy curl and tucking it behind her ear. 'You can't tell me you're tough. Not wearing that dress.'

Good grief. Good grief! How to cope with him looking at her like this?

There was only one way. Get back to practicalities—and get away from him!

'Yeah, well, this is a fairy-tale dress,' she told him. 'A once-in-a-lifetime fantasy. I've had my chance at playing the enchanted princess. Now it's back to being Cinderella.' She turned herself firmly away from him. 'Help me with these buttons, would you? There must be a hundred of the things.'

'Help you with your buttons?' he said faintly as she presented her back to him.

'That's the one,' she told him. 'Isn't that what husbands are meant for? Helping their wives undress?'

'Jenni, I'm...'

'Now, don't go getting any funny ideas,' she begged, fighting to keep her voice matter-of-fact. 'I'm wearing very respectable knickers and an even more respectable bra under this fantasy stuff. Not like the worn-out one I had on when Sam was injured. This is Home Brand, no-nonsense, even-your-grandma-would-wear-'em stuff. More respectable than a bathing costume, in fact. And there's no way you're unfastening that lot. All I want is a swim.'

'A swim...'

'I've been aching for a swim all day,' she told him. 'Longer. Since the fire. Yeah, okay, my hip hurts. And the best way I know to ease hurts is to swim.'

It was. It was the only way Jenni knew. She'd swum as a teenager when everything had crowded on top of her. She'd swum to ease the hurt of her parents' death, and when she hadn't known what to do. She'd swum when she'd been confused and frightened and alone.

She was confused now. She was confused right up to her eyebrows, so she stood rigid while William undid her buttons. The feel of his hands against her! Then, before he could say a word, or even take note of her respectable undies, she let her beautiful wedding dress fall on to the clean, golden sand and she took off towards the surf.

'Aren't you afraid of sharks?' William yelled after her, and Jenni shook her head, her curls flying free around her face. She should have braided her hair again. It still felt weird.

'Not me,' she managed as she reached the shallows. 'Besides, you said I was a mermaid. Sharks don't bother mermaids.'

'Says who?'

'It's a known fact,' she said scornfully. 'Mermaids just say boo—or call in King Neptune for the really heavy stuff. Like a school of manta rays with evil intentions. See you.'

And she launched herself into the waves, pushing her lithe body through one breaker and into the next, and then diving neatly into the third.

And disappearing from view.

William was left staring after her, her cloud of wondrous silk lying at his feet. And his world stood still.

He'd never met anyone like this girl. It was as if she really was a mermaid, he thought faintly. She'd cast off her human form and turned again into what she really should be.

Where was she?

He watched, suddenly anxious. She had a damaged leg. It was dark and there were night feeders. Stingrays. Manta rays with evil intentions?

She was tired.

Where was she?

And then she surfaced, far out beyond the line of breakers. The moon was glinting on the wetness of her hair. She raised her arm and waved—and then she put her head down and swam strongly along the back of the waves, parallel to the beach.

Away from him.

Good grief!

What to do here? What?

He should just slope off home.

He could do no such thing. If she got into trouble... She mustn't swim at night. Not alone.

This was madness.

She often did. He could tell that this wasn't a first, and the thought left him cold. No woman he'd ever met in his life before would do such a crazy thing.

Julia had been killed being crazy.

That was different, though. Julia's craziness was a world away from what Jenni was doing.

Was it?

Yes. Yes and yes and yes! Julia had been crazy for effect. She'd played her audiences to the hilt. For Jenni... Jenni was not playing for any audience here. She wasn't playing for him now. William knew if he took himself back home Jenni would keep on swimming. It was as if he no longer existed. She was a solitary swimmer, alone with her thoughts.

And she had manta rays and sharks and the odd giant squid to keep her company, he thought bitterly. And water snakes. And poisonous jellyfish.

His eyes would start glazing over if he didn't stop it.

'You've been in New York for too long, boy,' he told himself savagely. 'You're losing your touch. You used to swim here and you swam at night. No giant squid ever had you for a midnight snack.'

It looked so damned good.

Jenni looked so damned good. Her lithe form was cutting through the water like a dolphin. She must have been born to water.

She was almost more beautiful in the moonlight in the water than she'd been in her wedding dress.

'You should go home,' William told himself again, staring out at her, but he could no sooner turn and leave than he could fly.

So if he wasn't going home…

There was no way he was standing here watching a moment longer. It looked too inviting by far.

And she looked too lovely.

A man could only take so much. And he was married to her.

'She's my wife,' he said as he peeled off his dinner suit. He might still be as independent as he liked, but for now… 'Jenni's my wife.'

And suddenly the words sounded good. Fantastic, in fact.

This might be for only a year, but it was promising to be some year!

Out to sea, Jenni was thinking much the same.

In one long day her life had been turned on its head.

Not so much, she told herself firmly. Nothing's changed except you've got yourself a boarder.

You've got yourself a husband!

The thought was ridiculous. She glanced back at the beach to where William was standing watching in the moonlight.

He looked so…so alone.

He was as alone as she was, she thought suddenly. This man seemed so powerful and in control, but he'd hoed a row as bitter and hard as she had. Jenni knew there had been no joy for him after he'd turned sixteen—after his father had married Martha. Martha hadn't wanted him. Ronald had hated him and Ronald was criminally cruel. And then his father had died and he'd fought to take on the world by himself.

What William had faced wasn't so different from what she'd been through. Maybe he could say she'd had it harder because her sisters had been dependent, but then she hadn't been so alone.

Alone... He was standing there alone now, staring out to sea, and Jenni's heart twisted inside her. For the first time she didn't feel overwhelmed by his power or his good looks or his charm. For the first time she saw him as he really was—as he'd always been. Solitary.

William.

Her husband.

And then her breath caught in her throat as she saw him move. His coat came off first, and then the rest. All the rest, until he was standing naked in the moonlight. The moon shimmered on his magnificent naked body. Dear heaven, he was beautiful. He was so...so...

Well, for a start, he was so male!

And he was her husband! The thought made her go limp at the knees and she practically sank on the thought.

And then he was striding into the waves. Jenni could watch no more. There was no way she could tread water and watch and wait for him to come to her.

As of this evening, this man was her husband. This was her wedding night and yet...

Yet this was a business arrangement. This wedding was for a year, and a year only.

So get moving. He wants a swim and only a swim, she told herself, and she put her head down and started swimming again herself. As fast as her arms would take her. Away from William.

Away from her husband.

CHAPTER SEVEN

IT TOOK five minutes for William to reach her. Jenni was a strong swimmer and she'd had a hundred-yard start. Her head was down, and she was swimming strongly, but she felt him coming up behind her, and then swimming beside her, stroke for stroke.

He could reach out a hand and stop her any time he wanted, but he didn't. For a while he seemed content to keep pace with her.

Stroke to stroke.

It was a weirdly intimate experience. William was swimming between Jenni and the open sea. His presence beside her made her feel all at once protected—and very, very vulnerable.

Finally she had to pause. William might be able to keep up this pace, but not Jenni. It was her injured leg holding her back, she told herself, but she knew it was no such thing. William was too good.

So she stopped short and stayed where she was, treading water, while William sensed that she'd stopped, paused himself and swam back to her.

Now they were nose to nose in the water, with moonlight shimmering between them.

'You swim like a fish,' he told her, laughing, and Jenni smiled.

'You're not so bad yourself.'

'This is my home beach.' He looked around him with affection. 'I'll bet I've swum here more times than you,

Jenni. I swam every day from the time I was born until I was sixteen years old.'

'Since you were born...'

'My parents loved the water,' he told her. 'My first memories are of this beach. Of being held between my parents in the shallows.'

It was weird, talking as they were now. Weird and intimate and special. The whole ocean stretched before them but the scene was more intimate than any candlelit dinner. It was a night just for them.

'Do you swim in New York?'

That brought a cloud. 'No,' he told her.

'Why not?'

'I'm too busy.'

'What a shame.' Jenni grinned, breaking the intimacy. 'Then let's see. I've been here for ten years and you intend to spend one year here and then leave again. But I'm staying. So by the time I'm a hundred I'll have eighty-four years of swimming here and you'll have seventeen. So who's rich now, William Brand? Sometimes I don't feel poor at all.'

And she turned towards the shore, catching the next long, low swell and letting it carry her into the shallows.

William followed. Her wave slowed as it neared the sand, and William's was caught from behind by another. Jenni's wave veered sideways, pushed by the power of the two behind, so in the end he passed her, finding his feet in eighteen inches of water as Jenni surfed in beside him.

She almost bumped into his feet and he put down a hand to steady her.

She was just lovely!

She rose, dripping, in her plain white respectable knickers and bra, and with her lovely hair casting rivulets of water over her body.

She was right about her knickers and bra. Despite their

sodden state, they left everything to the imagination. Julia wouldn't have been caught dead in garments like this.

How could he talk her into buying something lacy? he thought. And then he gave himself a mental shake. Jenni didn't need anything lacy, he decided. She was lovely just as she was.

His hand held her as she steadied, but then he didn't release her.

He couldn't release her. Quite simply, he'd never seen anything—anyone—so beautiful in all of his life. She stood looking up at him, a half question on her face, and the urge to kiss her was almost overwhelming. The urge to take her…

His wife…

'William, we should go home,' she said, and there was a tremor in her voice. Well, how could she help that? He was naked, for heaven's sake. And he was so close! So close…

She tugged her hand but he didn't release it.

'William…'

Maybe this had been a mistake, she thought. To swim…

Maybe it had been a total mistake to marry. Because how could she stand here, and feel his hand holding hers, and not want him? Not ache for him?

She'd never known she could feel like this. Never! Something was happening to her and she didn't know what. Her legs were feeling odd. Her thighs…

There was heat starting in her body, radiating from her thighs and finding another centre right behind her eyes, but, despite the heat, she was trembling. And William's hold on her hand tightened.

'Jenni…' His voice was hoarse with passion. 'Jenni…'

It scared her to death. What was happening here? she thought. They were arranged in this seduction scene—dear heaven, she'd set it up herself!—and if it went its course…

All she wanted was for it to go its course.

But then… What then? Tomorrow…

Tomorrow, tomorrow and tomorrow, her heart whispered. Let me take them as they come. A year of tomorrows…

But then? After a year, what then?

Nothing.

So take what's on offer for now, her heart whispered. This man is your legal husband. Surely it can't be immoral to move a little closer. To let your body be pulled in to his…

To him. To William.

But then…

She closed her eyes and tried to speak, and her words came out a ragged whisper.

'William, we need to go home. This is…this is a business arrangement. Remember?'

And William shook his head, like a big wet dog, spraying water over them both. And suddenly he released her hand and changed position, moving to hold her with both his hands around the waist. Lightly. He pulled her forward and kissed her gently on the top of her head. And his words, when he spoke, could have been seen as lightly humorous. Light.

'This is the weirdest business arrangement I ever made,' he said. 'But you're right. We'll keep it formal. Despite the dress code.'

Light.

But Jenni heard what was behind the words. There was no lightness there, there was jagged, naked want. This was as hard for him as it was for her, she thought. Impossible. One day down, she thought desperately. One day down and a year to go.

So, without love, how long could a business arrangement last?

'Let's go, then,' he said, and released her abruptly to stride up the beach towards his clothes, and Jenni knew exactly what it had cost him to do that.

Because it had cost her the same.

Their business resolution lasted a whole fifteen more minutes.

That was how long it took for them to gather their clothes—for William to haul his trousers on to give him a semblance of decency—and to make their way up the beach to Kookaburra. Jenni kept on her knickers and bra. She really was respectable enough, she told herself, and she wasn't risking damage to Sally's lovely dress by putting it on again over her damp and salty body.

So they walked side by side up the track to the cottage, semi-clad and silent.

There were simply no words for what was between them.

There was nothing. The smallest crack and she'd break completely, Jenni thought. She was so aware of this man! Every nerve was aware of his body. Every sense was attuned to the sight of him. The smell of him.

William…

They were supposed to be staying in Kookaburra. Beth was staying with the Hayneses, and the arrangement was that Jenni could share the twin room in Kookaburra with Rachel and William could use the master bedroom.

So much for plans.

They reached Kookaburra and there was a huge note pinned to the door. Jenni read it by the light of the porch lamp. It took time to focus. She was so aware of William…

'Sorry, guys. Kookaburra is full. Mike and Ruby Lett are in the master bedroom here, fast asleep, so don't disturb them. Beth and Sam decided they didn't want to stay with the Hayneses, so they and Rachel are in the twin room. There's no room left. We've decided it's your wedding night so you're sleeping in Kingfisher.

Kingfisher…
Jenni stared. Kingfisher!

'So which one is Kingfisher?' William asked mildly, seeing nothing wrong.

'We're not sleeping in Kingfisher,' Jenni said. 'Mike and Ruby Lett are supposed to be sleeping in Kingfisher.'

'The note says they're sleeping here.'

'But they're supposed to be sleeping in Kingfisher.' Jenni's voice was practically a wail and William put a finger on her lips to motion her to hush.

'So they've given us a cottage of our own. Very thoughtful. We can hardly refuse, Jenni. How can we wake them now and tell them to go back to their cottage so we can share with the girls? Kick Beth out to sleep with the Hayneses again so we can have separate bedrooms? So much for pretending we have a real marriage.'

'But Kingfisher…'

'So what's wrong with Kingfisher?'

'It's the honeymoon cottage,' Jenni wailed. 'William…'

'So, okay…' He grinned '…it's only a name. Hey, Jenni, I can still sleep on the couch. Come on, before we wake up the whole camp. Which way?'

Jenni signalled to the last of the cottages, tucked away from the rest. 'But…'

'But nothing. Come on.'

And he took her hand and led her down the path. Brooking no opposition. The door to Kingfisher was unlocked. William pushed it open and tugged his bride inside.

And stopped dead.

Kingfisher…

Kingfisher had been the last cabin Jenni had built. She'd

built it after she'd had so many requests for a honeymoon suite that she'd felt she had to do something. It had been the last so she'd had the rent from the other cottages to indulge in more than second-hand furnishings and decor.

And they'd had fun with it. She and Rachel and Beth had giggled the whole time they'd built it.

It was a tiny, tiny cottage, and it was practically all bed. A timber-carving friend of Rachel's had carved the bed—the headboard adorned with hearts and doves—and they'd put two double mattresses side by side to fill it. Jenni had sewn black satin sheets and duvet covers. They'd put four satin-covered duvets on the bed so it looked like a vast mound of bedding, and there were cushions—scores of cushions, in every shade of the rainbow against the shining blackness of the bed.

There was a tiny table by the window overlooking the sea, and two cushioned chairs.

There was nothing else.

Just bed.

Oh, one thing more... There was a bucket on the table containing ice and a huge bottle of champagne. And a note. Jenni took a deep breath and walked over to read it. Ruby Lett had written:

'We honeymooned here four years ago and we've been back every year since. But tonight this bed is Mike's and my gift to you both. May it bring you as much pleasure as it's brought us.

And there was a postscript.

'P.S. The champagne's from Henry Clarins and the Betangera Rotary Club. Not that you two need it to get any happier!

William came up behind her, reading the note over her shoulder, and Jenni gasped as his chest touched her bare shoulder. She took off like a scalded cat to the other side of the bed, and spent three minutes carefully hanging her bridal gown and trying to ignore William. Trying to get her head back together. Or her heart…

'I guess I should hang up my dinner suit,' William said. 'But then, if I take my pants off I don't have anything on.' He looked sadly down at his bundle of clothing. 'I think I must have dropped my underwear on the track. How's that going to look to the early morning swimmers? Our reputation's shot.' And he grinned.

Jenni winced. She took a deep breath, and then turned and dived under one of the duvets. She hauled the satin covers up to her chin and tried to stop her knees trembling.

'You can't go to sleep in wet knickers,' William said.

'I'll take 'em off under the covers—on this side of the bed. You can do the same. On your side!'

'Yeah. Right.' William sat on the opposite side of the bed but made no move to take off his trousers. He lifted the champagne bottle. 'Drink?'

'N—no.'

'We should drink to our marriage.' Hell, why was his voice unsteady? *He* was unsteady! He poured a glass and held it out.

'No, thank you. I'm going to sleep.' She closed her eyes.

William took a long swig from the glass and put it back down on the table. Then he sighed, hauled off his trousers and got under the covers himself.

He'd never slept on satin in his life. It felt strange. Slippery and cool and…

'I'm not actually sure I like it,' he said into the darkness.

'What?'

'Black satin.'

'I think it's awful,' Jenni confessed. 'But Beth was all for it. She says black satin is what every honeymooner wants.'

'She's wrong,' William said. 'What every honeymooner wants is a wife. Or a husband.'

'William…' Jenni's voice was close to breaking-point.

'Jenni, I'm going to have to take a cotton duvet and sleep on the beach.' William groaned and writhed his naked body against the satin. 'Hell, Jenni…'

'We have a year of this.' Jenni swallowed. 'We have to get used to it.'

'Staring at the ceiling night after night?'

'That's right.'

'On opposite sides of the bed!'

'Different bedrooms from tonight,' she reminded him.

'Yeah. Ruby and Mike will want their honeymoon cottage back tomorrow.'

'I guess.'

'So it's only tonight,' he said. 'Jenni…'

'William.'

He was lying rigid on the far side of the bed from her. His body had never felt so tense in his life before. There were beads of sweat breaking out on his forehead.

No means no. If she says no…

But he wanted her so badly he could taste it!

'Jenni, do you remember me telling you I had priorities?'

'Yes. I think so…' Her voice was breathless.

'The first was not to marry. The second was to stop Ronald getting the farm. The third was to keep you safe.'

'I remember.'

'There's a fourth. And it's just launched itself to the top of my list.'

'And it is…?' Jenni's voice was a whisper. She knew what was coming. She knew!

His voice was an echo. 'And it is... You know what it is, Jenni. But... I'll sleep on the beach if you like?'

Silence. It went on and on and on.

Jenni's head was spinning. One part of her was cold to the core—trembling. Fearful.

The other...

He wanted her. He wanted her and he was her husband.

Well... So what? The sky wouldn't fall on her head if she moved to the centre of the bed. She'd promised to love and honour this man, and he'd made the same promise.

For a year?

Till death do us part, the vow had been, and that was what she was feeling now. As if her life would be changed for ever if she moved to the centre of the bed. But...not to move...

'William...'

'Jenni.' His hand came out and caught hers. And they lay rigid, staring at the ceiling with only the warmth of their hands linking each other.

And then William turned onto his side so his other hand could touch her. He put a finger on her lips and then moved his hand slowly down. Down across the smoothness of her throat. Down to where her breasts curved into two delicious peaks. He touched each nipple in turn, teasing, tantalising until each stood erect and hard and Jenni's body was starting to scream a need. Scream!

And then his hand moved downwards. Down across the flatness of her belly, and into the warmth—the heat—which lay between her thighs. His other hand released hers and gathered her against him, and there was no resistance. If she had resisted he would have stopped. He would!

But there was no resistance at all.

'My wife,' he whispered. 'Jenni, you're my wife. For a

year. We can resist this or we can run with it. We can have a year.'

'And…and then…?'

'Then life goes on,' he said unsteadily. 'But, Jenni… for a year…you're the sweetest thing. The most lovely… Jenni, right at this moment I want you more than life itself. That's all I can think of. At this moment… Now…'

And he pulled her gently into him so they were lying length to length. Skin meeting skin. And Jenni's toes were curling all by themselves.

This was crazy. Crazy! Dangerous, even.

What would happen at the end of the year? Could life simply take off where it had been left?

Jenni no longer cared. All she cared about was that William was holding her. She'd never known she could feel like this. She'd never imagined…

She wanted him. She wanted him and he was her husband. The moonlight was glinting in the window from the sea, and the night was theirs and they were man and wife.

And her arms came around and held him. In wifely possession.

'I could love you, William,' she whispered, and she let her lips drift up to touch his.

'Love me, then, Jenni,' he said softly, and his arms tightened around her lovely nakedness. 'Love me. Because I intend to love you. And I intend to love you right now.'

Dawn.

There was a kookaburra in the tree straight above the cottage. Its laugh was what woke Jenni and it had woken her husband before her.

She was curled tight into the crook of William's arms. He'd held her close even in sleep. They'd made love and

made love again, and Jenni had fallen asleep so happy she'd
felt her heart must surely burst.

She felt young and free and beautiful—and loved. She felt
protected and cherished. She felt as she'd never felt in her
life before, and she knew that if life ended right at this minute—if she woke to find William gone—then she could not
regret this night.

This night had been a gift from heaven. A gift to her.

But she woke and her husband was still by her side, holding her close, and when he spoke the tenderness and the
caring were still there.

'Damned bird. That's why I moved to New York. The
bird life here is enough to make a man demented.'

New York... The word sent a chill across the warmth of
the morning but there was laughter in William's voice and
the arms around her were tightening.

'The birds act as my alarm clock,' she told him.

'To do what?'

'To get up and start work for the day.'

'What about to stay where you are and start work for the
day?' He rolled over and up so that he was above her, looking down deep into her eyes. A man could drown in those
green eyes. 'I've just thought of something that needs doing.
Wife!'

'Wh-what?'

'Keeping your husband happy.'

'You mean...' her voice was a husky whisper. 'You mean
you.'

'That's the one. Your husband. That's me, Jenni, and I'm
so proud...'

And that was the last thing either of them said for a very
long time.

When she woke again, William was gone.

Jenni opened her eyes to find sunlight flooding the little

cottage. By the warmth and the power of the sun, it must be at least nine. She gasped and sat bolt upright.

Where was he? William's side of the bed was empty and barren.

He'd gone. He'd left her...

But there was a pile of clothing on his side of the bed. It was the dress they'd bought for her yesterday, and clean knickers and a bra. And a note.

'We're all over at Kookaburra. Come over when you're respectable, Mrs Brand. Love from Mr Brand.'

Jenni held the note and felt herself flush from the toes up. Mrs Brand.

'I guess I am Mrs Brand,' she whispered. 'Good grief!'

There was a party happening at Kookaburra. Half the occupants of the cottages were crammed into the kitchen or were spilling out onto the verandah. They greeted the flushed Jenni with warmth and laughter.

'Your husband's cooking breakfast, Mrs Brand,' they told her, and Mr Haynes gave her a wink.

'I'm glad the man let you sleep in. I went down for my early morning swim and what I found on the track... Well, I'm glad there was a legal wedding yesterday, and that's all I'm saying.'

And amidst more good-humoured laughter the guests on the verandah moved aside to let her into the kitchen.

William was indeed cooking. But so was Beth. There were pancakes being produced in industrial quantities.

'Okay, lift a spoonful of batter and let it run over your finger,' William was saying. 'Feel its texture. Remember it. That way you can just keep adding milk until you get it right. Okay, Beth, you cook this lot by yourself.'

And he turned from the bench to see his wife in the doorway. And his face creased into one of his wonderful smiles.

'Jenni.'

Goodness. If she hadn't known better she'd have said there was love in the word. There was certainly all the tenderness in the world.

Then everyone turned. There had to be twenty people in the kitchen, and at the centre of them all was Beth. She was flushed and happy, and she had the harnessed Sam at her feet. Beth put down the spatula she was holding and came towards the door, her hands reaching out to find her sister.

'Oh, Jenni…' Beth's voice was trembling with happiness. 'Can you believe it? I've cooked twenty pancakes. I burned four but the last twenty have been fine. I can time how long it takes for the pan to heat, and now I know how long it takes to flip them—and the last one I flipped without even using the spatula.' And she grabbed her sister and hugged.

Jenni closed her eyes. She had to—to try to stop the tears welling up. Useless attempt. 'Oh, Beth…'

Oh, William…

'Everyone's eating Beth's pancakes,' Rachel said, her voice almost as proud as Beth's. 'And she's prepared the second percolator of coffee herself.'

'I just have to make sure I have clean hands,' Beth told her. 'Because I feel everything. But, Jenni, I can cook. William can teach me. He's just the best.' She hugged Jenni hard. 'Oh, Jenni, I like your new husband.'

And Jenni's eyes opened, still sparkling with tears, and she looked over to where William was smiling at the pair of them.

Beth liked William.

It was no wonder. Jenni happened to like him herself.

It was the silliest, happiest day.

The cottage guests were all still in party mode and wanted

to extend the celebration. They decided as one that they'd do their own cleaning, thank you very much, and Jenni was left with nothing to do but enjoy herself.

'We should start cleaning out the fire damage from the house,' she tried, but was firmly squashed.

'We can't do that until the insurance assessors have been through,' William told her. 'For now…you're on your honeymoon, Jenni Brand. Forget your cares for a while. Just concentrate on being married.'

Concentrate on being married…

How could she do anything but concentrate on being married, when William's presence was so overwhelming? Her sisters loved him. The guests loved him. Even Sam showed his affection. Beth would always be absolute favourite with Sam, but the big Labrador was quite prepared to extend his friendship to include William as well as Jenni and Rachel.

'Even Sam thinks William's great,' Rachel whispered that night before she disappeared to study. 'Oh, Jenni, hang on to him. Keep him. This is the best thing…'

Hang on to him…

That gave her pause. 'Rachel, I'm not angling to keep him after a year,' she said, and Rachel shook her head.

'If you're not, then you're a dope,' she said. 'He's starting to be nuts on you, and anyone can see that you're nuts on him. And, besides, even if it is just for a year, then a year's a year, Jenni, and you've had no fun at all in your life until now. You go for it. Just take him and enjoy him for all he's worth. Year or not.'

And then night came and they were sent firmly back to Kingfisher.

'Because there's one honeymoon couple at Betangera and one honeymoon couple only,' Mike and Ruby declared. 'We're happy where we are, thank you very much. And it's giving us heaps of pleasure to know you're enjoying our satin sheets.'

But that night they didn't use the satin sheets.

They swam again, and then William took the cotton duvets down into the sandhills and they slept in each other's arms—with the roar of the surf in their ears and the warm sea breeze caressing them as they lay enfolded in a mist of love and desire.

And Jenni thought she'd died and gone to heaven.

How could it get any better than this?

This was heaven. A year of heaven?

CHAPTER EIGHT

THEY had three weeks of bliss. Three weeks of time out, where Jenni put her doubts and misgivings firmly aside.

This was a crazy relationship. She was mad to let herself love this man when there were no promises for the future and no commitment, but she couldn't help herself. No way! It was as if she were hypnotised.

William's presence did that. His looks. His voice. His laughter. The gleaming twinkle in the back of his eyes. The lust in his body. The way her body moulded itself to his, as if he was her home.

She'd break her heart when he left, she knew, but that was a year away. Anything could happen in a year. She didn't want to think about it.

The outside world was breaking in, but breaking in slowly. William made a string of telephone calls to his New York office, giving orders to his minions and asking for things to be sent—his computer, his fax machine and copiers and files...

His business life was on its way.

But meanwhile, before his New York life arrived, he was Jenni's. And her family's.

Beth was learning to cook more and more, gaining confidence by the day. She went back to school on the Monday with reluctance, and bounced off the school bus each night with pleasure. The pleasure was because William was there, and Beth could cook dinner for them all.

It wasn't just William's ability to cook that Jenni's little sister enjoyed. Beth's school taught her independence and

there were few things which limited her. The cooking was
a pleasure, but most of all... Most of all it was the sense of
family William gave her. With Rachel at university there
was usually only Jenni for Beth. Beth craved a family and
the child could hardly remember her parents. A large, solid
male presence was something new, and something special.

Jenni saw Beth's increasing devotion with a qualm. It was
one thing for Jenni to break her heart at the end of the year
when William went back to the US, but Beth was another
matter.

Even Rachel was falling under William's spell. The day
before Rachel was due to face her exams, Jenni found her
sitting on the steps outside Kookaburra while William took
her through her paces. William was reading from old oral
examination papers. Heaven, he must know nothing about
things like Guillain-Barré disease and circulatory paralysis
and tracheotomies, but he certainly sounded as if he did, and
his questioning technique—short and harsh and demanding—would prepare Rachel for the worst.

Rachel departed to face her exams with extra confidence,
thanks to William's help, and she hugged Jenni before she
left.

'I can't wait to come home at Christmas,' she confided.
'William's transformed this place. He's just the best thing,
Jenni.'

Jenni knew it.

It was an illusion, she told herself. William had her bewitched. He had them all bewitched, but all she could do
was enjoy it while it lasted. And try not to think about what
came next.

The insurance assessors did what they needed to, and then
Beth and Jenni and William moved back into the farmhouse.
Jenni had dreaded the work involved, but with William...
They worked side by side, hauling out damaged goods, re-

placing charred timber and cleaning the place from stem to stern.

After they'd cleaned out each room, they painted—a job Jenni usually loathed, but with William by her side it was fun. They ended up with more paint on themselves than on the house. It was a crazy, silly time and Jenni was falling deeper and deeper in love by the day.

They left the master bedroom—William's parents' room—until last, to be set up as William's office when his equipment finally arrived. Jenni's lean-to-cum-pigsty they transformed into a new bedroom. With a new bed...

A bed bought by William. And vast...

'Because if I'm staying here for a year, then I'm enjoying myself in the process,' he declared, and he put aside Jenni's protests and ordered a king-sized bed.

'What shall we do about sheets,' he asked as he leafed through a catalogue of fantasy bedding. 'I don't think I could stand satin.'

'I like fine linen,' Jenni told him grinning, 'or maybe silk would do nicely.'

She was teasing, but William paused over the catalogue and frowned. 'Silk... There's nothing here about silk sheets. Where can I get 'em?'

'I was joking,' Jenni said hastily. 'For heaven's sake, cotton's fine.'

'We don't really need anything at all,' William said thoughtfully. He made a lunge at her and hauled her into his arms. 'You're right, Jenni. Okay, no silk. No satin. How about the floor? How about now?'

Crazy, crazy, crazy.

And then, at the end of three weeks, the world broke in.

Thursday. Mid-morning. They were back living in the farmhouse, with William and Jenni in Jenni's lean-to on their ridiculous new bed. William and Jenni were painting the front porch, for once intent on their task and not each other. William was up the ladder and Jenni was painting the lattice at the side.

When the car pulled up Jenni didn't pause. Change-overs of guest was Saturday, so she wasn't expecting anyone. It was William who looked, and Jenni saw his face go rigid before she saw who their visitor was.

She turned, and it was Ronald.

'Good morning,' Ronald said urbanely, closing the door of his sleek black Jaguar and strolling towards them. He was looking his usual horrible self, still wearing his ridiculously expensive leather and with his hair even dirtier than last time Jenni had seen him. It was all she could do not to shudder. 'Quite the picture of domestic bliss, aren't we?'

'What do you want?' William demanded, not moving from his ladder. His voice was about as welcoming as iced water thrown straight in Ronald's face.

'I'm here for a chat. Aren't you going to ask me in?'

'Ronald, you're not welcome here,' Jenni told him, turning to face him square on. The anger in William's voice scared her. 'Not after what you've done.'

'What have I done?'

'This damage is down to you.' She motioned to the smoke stains still on the porch roof. 'Plus...' Her voice hardened. She knew what his worst crime was. 'You kicked Beth's dog. You nearly killed him.'

'And I'd do it again if I had a chance,' Ronald told her, smiling in remembrance. 'Stupid mutt. What a shame it didn't die. But I guess it was a bit crude. Not effective at all.' He took two steps back and stood gazing up at the house. 'Well, well. This is cleaning up nicely, isn't it? What a pity you're wasting your time. This place will be demolished in a month.'

'What do you mean?' Jenni asked.

Ronald wasn't allowed to answer.

'I've had enough of your threats, Harbertson.' William swung himself down from the ladder and placed himself between Jenni and Ronald. 'Go to hell. Get off this place. You're trespassing on our property.'

'On the contrary.' Ronald smirked. 'You're trespassing on mine.'

'Then you'd better tell us what you mean,' William growled. 'And hurry. I'm not into play-acting.'

'I mean that this place is mine.'

'And what are we supposed to make of that?'

'I mean I own this land.' Ronald looked over William's shoulder to address Jenni, cutting William out of the conversation as if he didn't matter at all. 'Jenni, my dear, this farm is yours only if you're legally married to my loving stepbrother here. And I'm desolate to inform you that you're not. You're not married. No matter what he's been telling you, your marriage certificate is worth less than the paper it's written on.'

'But... You saw us marry.' Jenni managed to speak, but she was suddenly breathless. She was afraid of what would come next. She knew it was something bad. Ronald's face was flushed with malevolent triumph, and he always had his reasons.

'You might have thought you were married, Jenni, my dear.' His voice was now mock sympathetic. 'But that's a nonsense. Because how can you marry a man who already has a wife?'

'A wife...'

'Is that what all this is about?' William said angrily. 'You've found some evidence—'

'Not *some* evidence,' Ronald said smoothly. '*The* evidence.' He reached into his top pocket and withdrew a piece of paper. With his eyes not leaving William's, he carefully unfolded it, and the malicious smirk grew wider. 'I have here a copy of a marriage certificate,' he said softly. 'For one William James Brand and Julia Maria Avetner. The marriage took place in New York eight years ago. And I've had my lawyers check the files. There's been no divorce. Has there?' His voice grew insistent and triumphant.

'No divorce at all,' he repeated.

And then there was silence. It went on and even the ocean seemed to still as it waited for William to respond.

Let him deny it, Jenni thought desperately, but William did no such thing. Finally—finally—he nodded and when he spoke his voice was flat and dead.

'No. There's been no divorce.'

'See? See?' Ronald's tone rose an octave. The man was almost beside himself with delight. 'You're not divorced, and nor could you be in the time stipulated by my mother for you to marry *her*!' He pointed to Jenni as if she were some repugnant form of lowlife.

'So you thought you'd con me,' he gloated. 'Ha! I've still got enough friends in high places to do my checking for me. You thought I wouldn't even bother to check. You're wrong. Your marriage is invalid, so now you can both get off my land. Now. And never come back. The pair of you.'

'Is that all you've found out?' William asked flatly. 'Is that all? That I married Julia?'

'It's enough. Why would I look for more?' Ronald sneered. 'Or have you any more wives hiding in cupboards? I only need one, you bastard, to get you off my land.'

'I only have one wife.'

'Yeah. And that's this Julia.' He waved the certificate again.

'No. My wife is Jenni.' And William reached behind him and took Jenni's hand. Tugging her forward, he placed his arm possessively around her waist and met Ronald's gaze head-on. 'This won't work, Ronald. Jenni's my wife. I'm no bigamist and our marriage is legal.'

'Then where did you get your divorce?' Ronald yelled. 'Cuba? A dash over the border to Mexico for a quickie divorce? That won't wash. I've checked with the authorities here. If you married in the States then you need to have registered your divorce in the States before the Australian authorities will accept it. You're still legally married.'

'I'm married to Jenni.'

'Then where's this Julia?'

'You haven't done your homework very well,' William said softly. His hold on Jenni tightened. 'You could have thought of the obvious. Why a man remarries. Only your mind doesn't work like that, does it, Ronald? It looks for corruption and deception and intrigue. There's no intrigue here. No deception at all. I'm married to Jenni, but you're perfectly right. I have been married before. But you should have checked more than just divorce records. Julia is dead.'

Again there was silence, and this time it was deathly. It wasn't a silence of waiting. It was the silence of shock.

Ronald's ground had been cut from under him and he was fighting to stand upright. Jenni could see his brain turn William's statement inside and out, fighting to reject something he desperately wanted to disbelieve.

William simply watched. His expression was calm and thoughtful. And patient. Waiting for Ronald to make another move.

And as for Jenni…

She stood within the confines of William's hold and she suddenly felt as cold as she had ever felt in her life before.

A wife… William had a wife? No. William was a widower. There had been…who? Julia?

'Take yourself off, Harbertson,' William said at last. 'Tell

your snooping little friends that they can search for the records of Julia. She kept her maiden name and was buried as
Julia Avetner so the records should be easy to trace. Julia
was killed at Aspen two years after we were married. That's
all you need to know. Now get off Jenni's land before I call
the police and have you carted away. It would give me considerable pleasure to do so.'

'You're lying,' Ronald growled, but Jenni could see by
his face that he didn't believe it. It was a forlorn hope. He'd
been so sure he'd win...

'I'm not lying,' William said. 'Now leave.'

There was nothing for Ronald to do but to leave. He did,
slamming the car door behind him and spinning the wheel
so the gravel blasted out behind him as he turned. It was a
futile protest.

Which left Jenni and William—to say what to each other?

It seemed William saw no need for comment. 'My paintbrush is drying,' he said, releasing his hold on Jenni's waist.
'I'd best get back to work.'

And say nothing? Jenni thought, stunned. As if what had
just happened was of no import at all?

Jenni closed her eyes. Maybe things hadn't changed for
William, but her world had just been given a monumental
heave.

'William, tell me about Julia.'

'What do you want to know?' he asked flatly, heading
back up his ladder. 'We met, we married and she was killed.
It was a long time ago, Jenni.'

'You didn't tell me.'

'No.' As informative as a brick.

'Aren't you supposed to declare it?' she asked carefully.
'When you marry? That you've been married before?'

'I did,' William said, dipping his paintbrush in the can
and starting to paint again. 'I put it in the forms we had to

fill out. You needn't worry, Jenni. I've told no lies. Our marriage is legal.'

And that was that. Jenni stared up at William's back but there was nothing more forthcoming. End of story.

So what to do? What was there to do?

Nothing. Jenni could think of nothing. She went back to work. William worked as steadily as before, but Jenni's heart wasn't in it. The joy had gone out of her day.

The bubble had burst.

Finally she gave up. She washed her brushes and came back to where William was still painting. 'I'm going for a walk,' she told him. 'I'll be back before Beth gets home.'

William looked down from the ladder, his face impassive.

'Are you okay, Jenni? Is something wrong?'

'I don't know,' she said carefully. 'I don't think it should be—but maybe it is. I just don't know.'

What business was it of hers that William had a wife before her?

Jenni asked herself the question over and over as she walked along the beach. She walked for miles, and every step she took she asked herself the question.

'What's between me and William isn't a marriage,' she told herself carefully. 'This is a business arrangement which has turned into an affair. It's the same as sleeping with the boss. Exactly the same.'

Oh, yeah?

Well, if it was, then she was head over heels in love with the boss. And she cared—cared deeply—that he should love her right back.

'It's gone too far,' she told herself. 'And why have I let it go so far? William never promised to love me. That wasn't part of the bargain. He's enjoying our affair. He's enjoying the novelty of this life, but he has another life—a life I know nothing of. For all I know, he really does have another wife in a cupboard somewhere. A wife and six kids on the other side of the world…'

Kids…

Good grief, if he'd been married then there might be children!

She knew nothing at all of William Brand. Nothing! And she'd imagined herself in love with him!

All she'd done was marry him and sleep with him—and let him take her heart as his own.

He was keeping his world apart, she knew. Look at him now! Painting on as if nothing had happened. He enjoyed what he was doing. He lived and loved for the moment, but he kept his life compartmentalised. His dead wife—well, that was six years ago so that wasn't to be thought of now. His businesses in the US… Jenni knew nothing of them.

And… His love life?

He had to have a love life, she told herself. William was too hot-blooded a man to have stayed chaste for six years.

So what?

So at the end of this year he'd go calmly back to his life in New York and to whatever women were part of that life. He'd divorce Jenni and she'd go into the Betangera compartment of his life— 'Oh, yes, I was married for a second time, but it was only for a year for business reasons and now we're divorced.' She could imagine him saying it to another bride somewhere down the track—with just as much unconcern as he'd dismissed Julia.

Oh, help. Where did she go from here?

Back to bed with William?

He wouldn't understand that she didn't want to. That she couldn't.

Jenni walked and walked, and it was only with reluctance that she finally turned to retrace her steps along the beach.

Beth would be home at five, and there were the accounts to be done and the dinner…

William and Beth would cook dinner. There'd be laughter and…

To her dismay, Jenni felt her eyes well with tears. Damn him, damn him, damn him! She kicked sand out in a spray before her.

Why was she so angry?

'He hasn't deceived me,' she told herself. 'He's saved the farm for me. I should be grateful.'

She wasn't angry at him, she decided. She was angry at herself.

'Because I'm a naive dingbat who's fallen for the first personable man who's drifted into my orbit,' she told herself crossly. 'So you can stop acting like a sex-starved spinster, Jenni Hartley. Jenni Brand. Whoever you are. Jenni Hartley. I'm still Jenni Hartley. So, Ms Hartley, you can get yourself under control, march him off to another bed tonight and take your life back to yourself again.'

Easy resolution.

She looked along the beach and William was walking toward her—and her knees turned to jelly.

Easy resolution. How on earth to keep it?

'Jenni?'

William came right up to her before he spoke. He'd obviously come to meet her.

Now what? How was she supposed to react now? she asked herself wildly. He was looking at her as if he didn't understand what on earth was going on.

Which he wouldn't, Jenni knew, and she understood why. He couldn't understand because William hadn't fallen in love. William had just taken what had been offered.

'I started to worry,' William told her. 'The Pride family

has arrived. I showed them into Mannagum. I hope that was where you wanted them. The beds haven't been made up but I told 'em we'd make them up later.'

Oh, help. The Prides. She'd forgotten they were expected.

She'd forgotten everything except the tumult around her heart.

'Jenni, why does the fact that I've been married before upset you?' William asked. Jenni hadn't paused as he'd reached her. She'd kept walking, and William had turned and fallen in beside her.

'It doesn't.'

'Liar.'

'It was just…Ronald scared me, that's all.' Jenni took a deep breath. 'And I can't help thinking,' she managed. 'Finding out about your wife made me realise… William, we're going about this all the wrong way. First we get married. Then we make love. Then we get to know each other. Only we still don't. Not at all.'

'I know you.'

'Well, I don't know you,' she burst out. 'And it's that that scares me stupid. Not Ronald.'

'You really do think I might have skeletons buried in my cellars?' His eyes twinkled down at her but there was concern behind the laughter. He really wanted to know what the trouble was. He really didn't see.

'No. Of course not.' How to explain? How to say that she loved him to distraction and the thought of there being parts of him other people knew and she didn't was unbearable. 'But…'

'Maybe I should have told you about Julia,' he said slowly. 'I just…'

'You thought it was none of my business. You're right. It's not.'

'It was all over a long time ago.'

Silence. They walked a hundred yards or more before Jenni spoke again.

'Is that why…when you met me you said you never wanted to marry? That not getting married was priority number one?' She caught her breath and then squared her shoulders. Forced herself to ask. 'Do you still love her?'

'What, Julia?' William gave a mirthless grin. 'Heck, no. No way.'

'Why not?'

'I don't think I loved her when we were married,' William told her, thinking it through as he spoke. 'Maybe I did, or maybe I just thought I did. I was infatuated, more like. I was twenty-six and I'd just made my first million. Until then I hadn't raised my head from survival mode. Suddenly the world was at my feet and Julia was, too. She belonged to a crowd I thought had everything. Money. Looks. Power. Only Julia didn't have money. Daddy had just gone bankrupt. So she made a play for me. I bankrolled Daddy, and Julia married me.'

He grimaced. 'So there. It's not such a different deal than the one we've made, is it, Jenni? The only thing was, I didn't understand that it was a deal. I was too young, too naive or maybe just too plain stupid. Julia was playing me for all she could get.'

'Oh, William…'

'Oh, don't feel sorry for me,' he said harshly. 'I learned soon enough. Keep the money coming, don't ask questions and Julia was happy. And don't get me wrong. The giving wasn't all one way. Julia gave me status. People came to my hotels who otherwise wouldn't. I became socially acceptable. And when Julia killed herself on the ski slopes— she was staying there with another man, by the way—I got sympathy from people I'd only ever read of in society pages.

Doors opened for me all over the place. So, you see, Julia's been useful.'

'As you've been useful to me,' Jenni said carefully.

'Well, maybe that's what marriage is for.' William smiled again then, and the self-mockery left his voice. He took Jenni's hand and held it up, as if inspecting her paint-spattered fingers. 'I made a vow then—to never leave myself open to humiliation again. Marriage can be useful, but if you manage to have fun along the way…as we're doing…'

He pulled her in close, as if to kiss her—but Jenni pulled back before his mouth touched hers. Her eyes were still troubled. She didn't understand this game. She was way out of her depth here, and once he started kissing her she couldn't think.

'No.'

'Jenni…'

'No,' she said again, and she found the strength to pull right back. 'William, I don't want this…'

His face stilled as he looked down at her. His hands still gripped her shoulders.

'Why?' he asked. 'Because of Julia? For heaven's sake, Jenni, that's crazy. Julia was years ago.'

'And I'm this year. And next year it will be someone else.'

'But we're married for this year.'

'That was the agreement,' Jenni said slowly. 'And I made it with my eyes open. And…I still need you, William. I still need to be your wife for a year.'

'So what's the problem?'

'The problem is the after,' Jenni said miserably. 'You see, I can't do this. I can't compartmentalise my life. Last year, this year and next year. For you, they're all separate. But for me they run into one another.'

'So…'

'So…if I'm not careful here, then I'll fall headlong in love with you,' she said.

Impossible to tell him she already had!

'And then… If I'm in love with you, then at the end of the year I won't let you walk away, William,' she managed bleakly. 'I'd cling like a limpet. I'd cling like I'd drown if you let me go. I can feel that already.'

She took a deep breath and looked up into his face. And his face told her what she needed to know.

'You don't want that,' she said softly. The thought appalled him. She could see it in his eyes. 'You want your life back after a year, so you can move on to the next thing. The next woman. The next business venture or the next country or the next…the next I don't know what.

'So unless you want me to be there, William, sharing your business, moving from country to country with you and fighting every other woman off with every weapon I possess, then we shouldn't take this any further. We went from being married to being lovers, to being acquaintances who knew nothing of each other. Let's just go back to being married. And that's all there is. Only a marriage.'

CHAPTER NINE

How to take the lover out of the equation and be left with a husband? How to stay living so close and yet separate? It was impossible.

What was worse, William didn't understand.

'Jenni, I don't see the difference,' he told her as she carted her things from the room they'd been sleeping in together. 'If I'd known it was important then I would have told you I'd been married.'

'It shouldn't have made any difference at all,' Jenni said crossly, hauling a heap of nightgear together. 'That's just the problem. It shouldn't, but it does. So for now I'll sleep in Rachel's bedroom. Tomorrow I'll start cleaning out the master bedroom so you can use that for the rest of the year. It has to be cleaned out anyway. Then I can come back here.'

'Come back to being a spinster.'

'That's right,' she snapped. 'I'm going to be one again at the end of the year so I might as well get used to it now.'

'Jenni, you didn't even want to get married,' he said, exasperated. 'Are you saying now that you don't want it to end at the end of the year?' His face softened a little and he walked across the room to confront her. 'Jenni, it doesn't have to. Not completely. We can still be friends.' He touched her chin, raising her face to his. 'Friends for life, Jenni. I hope we will be.'

Friends. Friends!

The man was so obtuse he was blinder than Beth, Jenni thought wildly. Friends. Ha!

'Look, leave it, William,' she said crossly. 'And don't try

138

to make me explain. Because I can't even explain what's going on in my head to myself! You can call me neurotic if you like. Explain it that way. You can call me anything you like, but I'm going back to being me. Not a part of you.' She heaved a pile of bedlinen into her arms and headed around him and out of the door.

'And tomorrow morning I'm going into town and I'm buying myself some blue jeans,' she flung over her shoulder at him. 'From now on I'm going back to being your wife in name only. And don't you dare try to act any different. Or...I'll even give Ronald his blasted farm.'

That night was a long night for Jenni, sleeping alone in Rachel's bedroom.

It was an even longer night for William.

He lay awake and stared at the ceiling and tried to figure out just where he was in all this.

He wasn't obtuse. He knew damned well what was happening here. Jenni hadn't come right out and said she loved him, but he could see what was written in her eyes. She'd described herself as naive. Well, she was. She couldn't hide what she was feeling.

So where did that leave him?

Playing the role of seducer?

He'd hardly made love to her against her will, he told himself harshly, and he knew it was true. She'd come to him gladly. She was ripe for loving.

The thought of Jenni's body, curled deliciously into his, yielding with delight to his touch, made him stir uneasily in bed, and he turned to stare at the wall between them.

The walls in this place were paper-thin. He could put out a fist and shove a hole between them. Through one lean-to into the other. Through his lean-to and into Jenni's. He could punch a hole big enough so he could stride into her bedroom, lift her into his arms and claim her back as his wife.

Only she wasn't his wife. Not really. She had the use of his name for a year, and that was all. If he claimed her now... If he claimed her now, then it would no longer be a bargain for a year. It would be a bargain for ever.

They never should have made love, he told himself bleakly. Jenni was right. It had just complicated the whole equation. Made it damnably more difficult.

But she was *so* lovely! And she was falling for him. She was falling in love, and she was afraid...

If she was falling in love with him then she should be afraid. There was no future down that road.

Because of Julia?

No. Because of what was important to him. His financial empire. His life! His need to be on his own.

Hell, why couldn't he sleep? Why couldn't he stop thinking? Why couldn't life just go back to being simple?

Breakfast the next morning was about as strained as it could be. Even Beth and Sam noticed the tension and Sam kept nosing his way from Jenni to William and back again as if he was trying to forge a link. As if he knew...

'So why did you sleep in Rachel's room last night?' Beth asked her sister as Jenni walked her out to the school bus. 'You two had a fight?'

'I always sleep in Rachel's room,' Jenni told her, blushing. 'You know that's what we decided we'd do. Until the master bedroom's cleaned out...'

'Are you kidding?' Beth turned to glare at her sister. 'It may be what we all agreed would happen but you two have been sleeping together for ever. Pull the other one, Jenni. You think I'm blind or something?'

'Now why would I think that?' Jenni smiled, but Beth wasn't being sidetracked.

'Me and Sam know what's going on in this place,' she said crossly. 'And you and William have been building a good thing between you. You're going to have to oil the bedsprings if you want to keep secrets from Sam and me.' Then, as Jenni's blush deepened, she went for broke, with typical fifteen-year-old candour. 'This was starting to feel like a real marriage,' she said. 'Until last night, that is. And I heard William tossing and turning, and I heard you howling your eyes out.'

'You did not!'

'I did, too. You don't survive blind if you don't grow big ears. And I use 'em. So what gives?'

'Nothing.'

'You mean…'

'I mean nothing. Beth, here comes the bus.'

'Well, fix things between you before I come home to-night,' Beth ordered. 'Make nothing something. Because me and Sam like the new order and we don't like it changing. We think William Brand is the best thing for you since sliced bread. So don't stuff it up, Jenni.'

And she gave her sister a quick hug and left her standing on the roadside, with Jenni wondering how on earth she could possibly obey that order.

Don't stuff it up?

What was there to stuff up?

Nothing. There had been nothing from the start.

Beth wasn't leaving things there. That night she probed Jenni relentlessly until she had all the information she could muster. Then she waited until Jenni was called out to one of the cottages—Mrs Fairhurst's open fire was smoking—and launched into an inquisition.

She started tactfully. Gently. Like bull-in-a-china-shop gently.

'So why aren't you sleeping with Jenni any more?' she demanded of William. 'And why are you hardly talking? Don't you love her any more?'

William was mid-wash while Beth was wiping the dishes dry. He practically dropped the casserole dish he was scrubbing. Hell, he wasn't used to the directness of teenagers.

'Is this...is this any of your business?' he managed, and started scrubbing again.

'No,' Beth admitted. 'But I'm asking anyway. And you can't tell me to butt out. I'm blind.'

'Now, what's the reasoning behind that?'

'You're supposed to feel sorry for me and give me what i want. Like information.'

'Says who?'

'Says me.' She grinned. 'Otherwise I'll have Sam lick you until you scream for mercy.'

'You see me petrified.'

'So tell me.'

'No.'

'Jenni says you've been married before.'

'Beth...'

'To someone called Julia. Do you still love her?' Beth carefully accepted the casserole dish from William and started wiping. 'If she's been dead for six years you can hardly still love her.'

'I don't.'

'But she's still affecting you. Mind...' Beth sighed and stared into the middle distance '...I can imagine she would. Dying young... It's so romantic to die young.'

'It wasn't romantic at all.'

'No.' Beth caught herself, romance making way for reality. 'I guess not. When my mum and dad died it was dreadful. Empty. And then...well, I lost my sight in the same accident. I was only five but I still remember the feeling. Like everything was empty. Black and empty. Awful. There was just...just nothing.' She blinked. 'Was it like that with you? When you lost Julia?'

William paused. He couldn't tell her to butt out now. With Beth's confession of devastation, the questioning had become much more intense...much more personal. But she wasn't prying. She was asking him to share a part of himself, as she was sharing.

'I don't...'

'Did you feel that?' Beth probed. 'That emptiness?'

'I guess I did,' William said, finally letting himself think back to those days following Julia's death. The haunting images of Julia's shattered body. The searing hurt of the dream finally ended.

'And do you still?'

'No...'

'You try not to think about it, but it's there,' Beth said softly. 'Isn't it? It never really goes away. The feeling that everything you have can be taken away.' She blinked and blinked again, and Sam came up behind her and licked her palm. He was a very sensitive dog.

'I don't think it's fair to compare what I felt for Julia to what you felt for your parents.'

'But you did love Julia?' She sighed. 'Of course you did. Even if you were fighting... Even if you were unhappy before she died, you were still married to her. When you marry someone...you marry a dream. I know. I get the romance novels from the Braille Library. And then reality sets in but the dream's still there. And then...you'd only been married for two years, Jenni said. No matter how she was killed...'

'Beth...'

'I'm sorry. I shouldn't stick my oar in like this,' Beth

agreed. 'It's only…you see, Jenni hasn't had a dream. Ever. Since Mum and Dad died and I was so dreadfully injured…well, all Jenni's had has been duty. Me and Rachel. But then…' She looked earnestly at William, as though she could see him. Willing him to understand. 'But then you came along. And you've only been here for three weeks, but I know Jenni's now been given a dream. But you… If your dream's still your dead wife…'

'It's not.'

'But…because of Julia you're not dream-hunting,' Beth probed. 'You're not about to put someone in her place. Someone like Jenni.'

'Beth, I'm being practical. Jenni doesn't want me as a long-term husband.'

'Have you asked her?'

'No, because…'

'Because you don't want a long-term wife. Why not?'

'Because…'

'Because you're still hung up on Julia,' Beth said triumphantly. 'You are. Aren't you? So admit it.'

'I'm not.'

'Yeah? If you hadn't married Julia, would you be feeling the same way you are now? Like you never want another relationship? Isn't that because of Julia?'

'Maybe, but—'

'Maybe nothing. Maybe definitely.' Beth abandoned her tea towel. She hauled herself up backwards to sit on the kitchen table, her schoolgirl legs dangling. 'So we need to vaporise Julia. How do we do that?'

'Beth…'

'Think of a way,' she said urgently. 'William, Jenni needs you. I'm blind, but I can see that sticking out a mile. She needs you.'

'She doesn't.'

'Then I need you,' Beth snapped. 'I need you as a brother-in-law. Doesn't that count as anything?'

'Beth, it's flattering, but—'

'But you don't want to be needed,' Beth said crossly. 'Well, you are. So stick that in your pipe and suck it, Mr William Brand. This family wants you and needs you and we need you for more than a year. So shove your selfish dreams of the lovely Julia and get on with living. Give a bit. Jenni gives and gives and gives. It wouldn't hurt you to do the same.

'And now…if you'll excuse me, I have homework to do,' she said. 'The way I'm feeling…well, you can finish the washing up all by yourself. All of it. Goodnight.'

And she slid herself off the table, stalked to the door and whistled to her dog to follow.

'It's coming to something when the only male you can love is a dog,' she said bitterly. 'Get over it, William Brand. Quit pining for what's lost. Get a life.'

She waited for Sam to pass through the door, and then she slammed it behind her.

'What's Beth been saying to you?'

'Sorry?' William had been a million miles away. He was standing on the verandah staring over the ocean, and Jenni's voice made him start.

'I've just been in to say goodnight to Beth,' Jenni said softly. 'She said she gave you a piece of her mind.'

'She did at that.' William didn't turn. He stayed where he was, watching the moonlight on the sea.

If he turned…

He was so close… So close to doing what Beth suggested. So close to letting himself fall for another dream.

When he'd thought of this plan he hadn't counted on Jenni

being so...so damnably desirable. The last three weeks had
been wonderful. Holding her... Making love to her...

So why couldn't he take it further? Encourage the love
and trust he saw in her eyes? Take away the end point of a
year and say they had a marriage—let it end when it would.

Impossible. It was impossible to let go of the armour he'd
built up in the years since he'd married Julia. His life was
his work and his friends. He was independent and he liked
it that way. Hell, what happened when you committed to
someone?

He'd loved his mother but she'd died.

He'd loved his father but Martha had elbowed in and
turned him out. Left him heartsick and lost.

And then Julia... He'd thought he loved her. He'd let
himself need her. And the same thing had happened.

And now...

If he took this further...if he let Jenni's sweetness envelop
him...?

Maybe she wouldn't hurt him, but then... Could he promise not to hurt her?

His life wasn't here. It was in New York. It was international. He couldn't give up his financial empire. So he'd
spend most of the year travelling, come back to Jenni every
now and then and give her a part of him.

He'd hurt her. He wasn't capable of giving the sort of
loving she deserved.

'William, when you offered to marry me...' Jenni said
carefully behind him, and heaven only knew the effort it
cost him not to turn '...you made a bargain. The pressure
Beth and I are putting on you now is unfair. You're playing
your part of the deal. So whatever Beth said... Ignore it,
William. We got on very well without you and we'll get on
without you again. You'll be able to walk away from us at
the end of the year, and I promise I won't let Beth blackmail

you emotionally again. We'll leave you be, William. I'm sorry.'

And she turned and walked back into the house, leaving William to his thoughts.

Fine!

Only why were those thoughts just *so* bleak?

A year was starting to seem a very, very long time.

The next day was Saturday. Beth was off school. The tension between the three of them was palpable over breakfast, but they were determined to make an effort to be businesslike.

At least, Jenni and William were determined to be businesslike. Beth was just plain cross.

'You're a pair of dopes,' she told them. 'I told you to sort it out, and you still slept apart.'

'And we're sleeping apart from now on,' Jenni told her sternly. 'Beth, keep your oar out of what's not your concern. Now... Rachel's due home for the summer on Wednesday. I want to be out of her room by then. That means we need to clean out the master bedroom to set it up as William's office and bedroom.'

'It's ridiculous.' Beth sniffed. 'If you ask me, it's a waste of a perfectly good love affair.'

'Well, no one's asking you.' Jenni flushed and refused point-blank to look at William. 'Beth, will you help us clean?'

'No.'

'Fine. Suit yourself.'

But in the end she did. They all did.

The farmhouse master bedroom had hardly been touched in years.

'Dad hadn't been remarried for more than four weeks before Martha declared she wasn't living here,' William told them, looking around the room with bleak, remembering eyes. 'They rented in town until they bought the new house. Martha wanted this place let, but my father wouldn't. He always said he'd leave the place for me and he didn't want strangers in it. It was my bolt-hole until I left home.'

'So why didn't he leave it to you?' Beth asked curiously, fingering the ancient bedspread. Jenni had kept this room clean, but she'd left it as she'd found it. Nothing had been moved.

'He did—in his old will,' William said. 'But his remarriage invalidated that, so Martha got the lot.'

'It must have hurt—that your father didn't remake his will,' Jenni suggested softly, watching his face. There was so much about this man that she didn't know—that she wanted to understand.

'As you say.' His face was closed now. But Jenni knew just how hurt that eighteen-year-old had been. To have been left with nothing...

How much of this man's cool independence was the product of that hurt? And the hurt the unknown Julia had inflicted...?

Her fingers were curling into claws. Jenni took a deep breath and got a hold on herself. He wasn't asking for pity. William wasn't asking for anything at all from her. He'd made that perfectly clear.

'Okay. I've done superficial cleaning but that's all,' she said, keeping her voice brisk and efficient. 'Let's strip the lot. Get everything outside. I think the soft furnishings will disintegrate when we touch them but that's a risk we have to run. Beth, can you and Sam haul the bedclothes and the curtains and the rugs outside? Hang them over the line and beat the daylights out of them, and I'd cover your mouth while you do or you'll be sneezing for a month. William, you and I get to cart the big stuff out.'

'Yes, ma'am.' William gave a smart salute but there was no smile behind his eyes. This was hard, Jenni knew.

The whole situation was hard. Impossible.

It became even trickier fifteen minutes later. Jenni found William's father's will.

The document was taped to the underside of the bedside chest of drawers.

Jenni was sitting in the sunshine where they'd dumped the furniture so the room could be thoroughly scrubbed. She was progressively removing each drawer, holding each upside down and emptying out the detritus of long years of disuse. The drawers had been emptied eighteen years ago and hadn't been touched since.

Beth was sneezing in the background while she pounded the rugs with a broom.

William had started scrubbing down walls. The smoke had got in there, and had to be removed if they were to paint.

Jenni turned over the drawer, saw what was underneath and frowned. It was a long white envelope, taped to the underside. It wasn't labelled.

Curiously she lifted it from the wood, the paper crumbling at the sides from long contact with the tape. It wasn't sealed, and what was inside was almost as fresh as the day it had been placed there. She flicked it open and stared.

'I, John Raymond Brand, being of...'

Good grief.

Jenni stared down at it, bemused. What had William said about his father's will? He'd made one once, but his marriage to Martha had invalidated it.

So when was this made?

She stared at the date, and then started doing fast calculations. She wasn't sure of dates, but this had to be close to the time Martha and William's father were married. Very close.

So...

She shouldn't look further. It was none of her business.

There was no way in the wide world she could stop herself looking now. The will was simple. Two pages of handwritten instructions. Witnessed...

Who had witnessed it?

Jenni stared at the names but they meant nothing to her. They weren't locals.

But what did it say?

Her eyes were skimming fast, and she was hardly daring to breathe. What...?

> To my new wife, Martha, I leave my share of the jointly owned home in Betangera Bay, my personal possessions and all my personal fortune.

But William...William! Surely he hadn't abandoned William!

And there it was.

> To my son, William, I leave Betangera Beach Farm. If I die before William comes of age, I wish the farm to be let and the proceeds used to pay for his education and keep. All income from the farm will go to him absolutely. On his twenty-first birthday, the farm is to be William's, to do with it as he pleases.

Jenni's breath let out on a long, long gasp. She rose to her feet, trying to take in all the ramifications of what lay in her hand. She couldn't.

All she saw in that first instance was that some of the hurt she saw behind William's fear of commitment might now be eased. His father hadn't abandoned him on his new marriage. His father had remade his will.

'William,' she yelled, and she yelled so loud it was as if the place were on fire again. 'William!'

He came running. Jenni saw his fear of what Ronald might still do as he burst out of the door, and his face slackened in relief as he saw her safe. He slowed to a walk, and reached her as Beth and Sam came tearing around the side of the house.

'What's wrong?' Beth was calling frantically. 'Jenni, what's wrong?'

Unlike William, Beth couldn't see that Jenni was fine. That there was nothing wrong at all. That she was standing in the sunshine with a sheet of parchment in her hand and a strange expression on her face.

It was an expression she couldn't figure out herself. There were two emotions warring within her now.

One... If the farm was William's, where did that leave her? Where did that leave Beth and Rachel?

The second was different, though, but increasingly it was the overriding one.

This document in her hand meant that William hadn't been forgotten. His father had put his will somewhere safe and then he'd forgotten it, but he'd made it all the same. After his remarriage, he'd still remembered he had a son.

'It's okay, Beth,' Jenni said quickly. 'I've just found something...a paper...taped under a bedside drawer. It's...it seems rather important. I think William really needs to see it.'

And she handed over his father's will and waited for William to read it.

The silence was deafening.

Beth didn't have a clue what was going on, but she was an intelligent child. She knew it was something major. So she stood, her hand on Sam's harness holding him still, while Jenni watched William's face. While he read.

William read it three times. Over and over. And at the end he let his hand fall and he stared sightlessly out to sea.

'It's dated the third of June,' Jenni said gently. 'When did they marry, William?'

Nothing.

'William?'

He turned to face her then, his face blank with shock.

'When, William?'

'The fourth of May,' William told her, his voice devoid of any expression. 'Four weeks before this was written. This was made just after they bought the house in Betangera Bay, but before they moved there. If this is valid...'

'I'll bet it is.'

'If it's valid...'

'Then you own this farm,' Jenni said gently. 'Ronald's never had any claim on it at all. And neither have I.' She caught her breath and fought for courage for what she had to say next. 'It's finally as it should have been all along. So it seems...it seems you've married me for nothing, William. The farm is yours. We'll...we'll rent it from you, if you like...the same as we did from Martha. But... But if you want us to... Then we'll leave.'

CHAPTER TEN

WHAT do you mean—leave?'

It was Beth. Of course it was Beth. The child was totally bewildered, not understanding a word of what was going on.

Jenni dragged her eyes from William's face with an almost superhuman effort.

'You know we've always said it was odd William's father didn't leave William the farm,' Jenni managed. 'I've just found his will. It seems he did. Of course he left the farm to William, so it was never Martha's to leave to anyone at all. Martha had no right to leave it to Ronald and she couldn't leave it to me. It never belonged to Martha, and now it belongs to William.'

'But...but why didn't we know about it?' Beth's voice rose in bewilderment. 'Don't you have to make a will with a lawyer or something? How can you just...just find it?'

'You can write a will yourself, without the help of lawyers.' Jenni's eyes had swung involuntarily back to William, watching as the importance of what she'd found sank home. He looked as if he'd been struck. Hard.

'And there seem to have been two independent witnesses, so the will's probably legal,' she went on, her eyes not leaving William's. She shook her head, thinking it through as she watched the blank incredulity in William's eyes. 'He must have forgotten to lodge it somewhere safe. William...'

'He won't have thought of it.' William gave a bitter laugh. 'Hell, he won't have thought of it. My father was the original absent-minded professor. My mother did his organising, then I did and finally Martha took over. He'll have come back from getting married and changed his will and then not thought about it again. Though…why on earth he taped it under the drawer…'

Then he shrugged, deep in thought. 'Maybe even then he saw how domineering Martha was. That if Martha knew he'd made such a will she'd nag until he changed it. So he hid it. And then he'll have forgotten all about it. It was important until he'd written it, and then it wasn't urgent any more. So lodging it with a lawyer didn't get done.'

More silence. Even Sam seemed to be thinking this through.

Then…

'So if it's your farm now, William,' Beth said, in a scared little voice, 'will you…will you want us to go away?'

That got to him. Beth's shock and fear reached through his own shock, and snapped him out of it. He looked at Beth and he looked at Jenni, and there was fear on both of their faces.

Fear!

What on earth could they fear? His face creased into a grin as finally the enormity of this document hit home. The joy! He'd been so hurt when his father had died. First there had been the shock of losing his father, and then the real-isation that his father had left him nothing. The feeling of absolute abandonment had stayed with him ever since.

And now this!

He gave a shout of delight, grabbed Beth and whirled her around until Sam barked with excitement. And then he put Beth down and grabbed Jenni. She didn't yield to him as she'd have done only days before, but he didn't release her. He swung her body around and held her.

He hugged her hard, and heaven only knew the effort it cost Jenni not to hug him back. To hold herself apart.

She must! Because her whole being was waiting for what would come next.

Finally he put her down.

The delight on his face wasn't reflected on Jenni's, he thought, wondering. She looked wooden—as if she was expecting to be struck.

'Hey, I'm not putting you off the farm, Jenni,' he said quickly. 'No way in the world. But it's mine. If this will's valid, then there's no way Ronald can touch it. My father gave it to *me*!' He said the words in a triumphant shout. And then he paused.

He took Jenni's limp hands between his. His voice gentled. The fear was still there on her face, and all of a sudden he couldn't bear it. In the last few moments, his world had become wonderful. A pain which had been with him for so long had been lifted like magic. And this woman had given him this gift.

He could give it back. *He could give it back!*

'The farm's yours, Jenni.'

'What…what do you mean?' It was as much as Jenni could do to manage a croak. She took a huge breath and fought to collect herself.

'I mean I'm giving it to you.' He held up the document as if it were more precious than diamonds. 'I'll take this in to Henry Clarins right now and have him check it. Have him track the witnesses. But if it's right… Then it's my wedding gift to you, Jenni. Or my divorce gift. Whatever. It's over. Ronald can't touch it. He can't touch you. It's over.'

'And then you'll leave?' Jenni said slowly. All she heard were those two words. Like a death knell. *It's over.*

'There's no need for me to stay.'

'No.'

Of course not. She was being stupid here. Stupid and sick at heart.

But she knew what she had to do. One thing at least was clear.

'You're not giving the farm to me, William,' she said, and somehow she made her voice sound almost normal. Conversational. 'I'm not taking your farm.'

'Jenni…'

'I'm not taking it.' Jenni crossed to where Beth was standing, and she took Beth's hand. She linked herself to her sister as if she could draw strength from her. 'Beth will agree with me, and so will Rachel when she knows. We don't take charity. Sure, we've accepted help from time to time—we've had to, but we've accepted only small things. Only things we could repay with offers of accommodation or straight friendship. But this is something else, William. This farm is yours. If you'll agree to Martha's terms then we'll stay renting it from you, but that's all. All, William.'

'Jenni, don't be stupid.'

'I'm not being stupid,' she said flatly. 'You married me to give me the farm, and I agreed to that. But that was only because otherwise Ronald would have it, and he deserved it even less than I did. This is different. Your father wanted you to have the farm. It's yours.'

'You're my wife, Jenni,' William said, watching her face. 'My father would have wanted my wife to share it.'

'Share, yes—if I really was your wife. But I'm not. You're not talking of sharing the farm here, William. You're not talking of sharing anything. Especially not your life.' She closed her eyes, pain washing through her. 'I'm not your wife, William. Go back to the States. I'll file for divorce, and then you can go back to being free. Being whoever you are in your other life. And we'll get on with being us.'

'Jenni, you must keep the farm.'

'You can rent it to us,' she said dully. 'If you're a better landlord than Martha, then we'll be grateful. But that's all.

You've given us enough, William. Enough. Now it's time to move on—back to our separate lives.'

She wouldn't budge for a moment.

William spent the next three days arguing with her, in turn demanding, threatening and pleading. She wouldn't listen at all.

And Rachel and Beth, when appealed to, took Jenni's side with a vengeance.

'Our Jenni always takes the moral high ground,' Rachel said when she arrived home from university. 'You can't make a silk purse from a sow's ear. I don't think it's Jenni's style to be a kept woman.'

'Damn it, I'm not paying her to be my mistress.'

'No,' Rachel said thoughtfully, swinging her long legs on the porch swing. She'd been home for twenty-four hours now, jubilant after passing her exams and with her hair dyed crimson. She'd looked carefully at the strain on Jenni's face and she'd listened to what Beth had to say and she'd come to her own conclusions. 'I'm starting to think the opposite. I'm starting to think you're paying her *not* to be your wife.'

'Now what's that supposed to mean?'

'You didn't even know Jenni when you came home a month ago,' she told him. 'You'd met her briefly when you were kids and you hadn't contacted her for years. Then, in the space of a few days, you met her, you married her and you made love to her. And you made her fall in love with you.' Then, as his eyes snapped into a frown, she held up a hand to silence him. 'Look, maybe I'm wrong. This is all according to Beth, but you can't fool Beth. She doesn't just have a sixth sense to compensate for her lack of sight. She has a seventh, eight and ninth sense as well. She says Jenni's head over heels in love with you, and I believe that. But you don't want it. So you're giving her the farm.'

'That's not it.'

'So why are you giving her the farm? She's happy to rent it from you.'

'She needs it. I don't.'

'Nope.' Rachel hauled herself off the swing and picked up her beach towel. She was now officially on summer vacation, and she was making the most of it. 'You know what I think? I don't think Jenni needs a farm. I reckon she needs you. And Beth says you need her too,' she added conversationally. 'I don't know about that, but I have enormous respect for Beth's opinion. But even if she's wrong you must see that if Jenni's in love with you it would break her heart to have to take your pay-off. Your farm—but nothing else from you.'

'I don't see it.'

'Then you're blinder than Beth,' Rachel said kindly. 'Open your eyes, William Brand. Open your eyes and look. Only I don't think you're blind. I think you're just set in your ways. Open up a little. Live a little—and let yourself love.'

Damned kids. If this was what having a family was all about then he was glad he'd never had brothers and sisters. They were too direct for comfort.

Too truthful?

All William's office equipment had arrived the day they'd found the will. Now it all had to be repacked and redirected back to the States. William worked on a pile of packing cases and tried to ignore the sound of laughter coming from the next cottage. There was a possum on the roof. Sam was turning himself inside out trying to climb the trellis on the porch, and the girls were egging him on.

Unconcerned, the possum sat on the ridge of the roof and washed his face.

Five days ago William would have strolled over to watch. Now... He felt out of it. Old.

No longer one of the family.

Which was just as well, he told himself firmly. He didn't like having little sisters chastising him. Taking the moral high ground. Especially when they were wrong!

Then Sam made a spectacular leap at the trellis and managed to grab a hold about four feet up. His hind feet got a grip and he shoved himself higher. Six feet and climbing...

The rose cane holding him swayed outward. The big dog sagged sideways and he started falling—and Jenni shoved her slight body forward to break his fall.

Before he could stop himself, William was taking fast steps forward, breaking into a run as dog and girl fell sideways and landed in a tangle of legs and tail and laughter.

Six strides...then Jenni's face appeared over her armful of dog, and her eyes were brimful of gaiety.

'Oh, you stupid dog. You deserved to fall. Ouch! Beth, don't they teach dogs how to climb at seeing-eye-dog school?'

She rose, hauling the dog up with her, and half turned. Then she saw William only twenty feet away. The laughter died out of her face as if it had never been.

'Take your dopey dog, Beth,' she told her sister. 'I don't know what I'm doing here. Some of us have work to do.'

And she disappeared into the house, closing the door behind her.

'Did you want something?' Rachel asked William politely, and her mere politeness excluded him absolutely. He wasn't one of them. And—what was worse—he was hurting Jenni. Rachel's eyes accused him and condemned him all at once.

Beth and Rachel and Sam stood as a united front between him and the door. Between him and Jenni.

'No. I thought Jenni might be hurt.'

'Even if she was,' Rachel said coldly, 'it's up to us to fix that now. It's not up to you.'

Hell!

It had to end and it had to end now. That afternoon William took himself off to visit Henry Clarins and, when he returned, he had finally sorted out what he intended to do.

Rachel and Beth were swimming. Jenni was sitting on the roof of the farmhouse, staring sightlessly out to sea. When she saw William's car returning she started work again, furiously banging on loose shingles.

Seeing her working like that made his heart twist. She shouldn't be working so hard.

'That's the landlord's job,' he called up to her. One thing he could do was take over paying someone to do maintenance. 'I'll get Henry to organise someone to come on a regular basis.'

'It's going to rain tonight,' Jenni told him. 'You got a maintenance team prepared to shingle right now?'

'I'll help.'

'I don't need help.'

Yeah. Right.

She didn't move. She stayed up on her roof banging as if her life depended on it, and he thought suddenly that this was how he'd remember her.

Alone...

Why couldn't he commit himself here? he demanded of himself. Why couldn't he storm up that ladder, take the hammer out of her hands and kiss her...?

She had a mouth full of nails for a start.

But that wasn't the only reason. They were poles apart, he thought as he stared up at her. She was wearing her blue jeans again now with a vengeance. The lovely clothes he'd bought her were locked away, and he suspected they'd never see the light of day again. For a little time—a short sweet while—she'd played with being William's wife. Now she was back to being Jenni.

And he didn't want William's wife, he thought suddenly. He wanted Jenni—in fact his loins were starting to throb just thinking about it! Just looking at her.

'I need to talk to you, Jenni,' he told her.

'So talk.' She was talking out of one side of her mouth, holding her nails with the other.

'I'll crick my neck.'

'I can't come down. These have to be finished by tonight.'

'I'm leaving.'

That gave her pause. She stopped and looked down at him for a long, long moment, taking her fill. Then she carefully removed the nails from her mouth.

'I...I guess it's time,' she said.

'Jenni...'

'I hate goodbyes. Hate 'em. Can't you...can't you just go? Do you really want me to come down this ladder and shake hands?'

It wasn't what he wanted. He wanted her to come down the ladder and be kissed. He needed to kiss her goodbye. But then...

It wouldn't end there, he knew. If he held her again...

If he felt like this, what in earth was he doing leaving?

He couldn't stay, he told himself, and his reasoning was ragged. He was hardly making sense to himself. But his life was on the other side of the world.

He was an international businessman and he didn't need to be told that Jenni would hate the sort of life he led. She'd be desperately lonely. He worked long hours. How could she cope with his fifteen-hour days? How could she live with corporate entertaining and with weekends that didn't exist?

His world wasn't hers, and her world was no longer his. He had a financial empire to run, and staying here just dragged out the pain of leaving.

He looked around him, and he felt his gut twist in regret. Jenni's world had once been his, but he couldn't come back here now. Not permanently. For heaven's sake, this was the end of the world. The southern tip of Australia! You couldn't make money here. Jenni was eking out an existence, but she'd never be rich.

Sure, it was her home and she loved it as she loved her sisters. She'd go on living here, but it was time for him to move on.

Back to his life.

His thighs tightened again, and he almost groaned. His body was giving him messages that his head couldn't comprehend. His body wanted him to stay.

Yeah? Just because of a woman? To abandon a financial empire for a year was one thing, but for ever?

Get out of here, Brand, he told himself. Get down to the beach and say goodbye to Beth and Rachel—and then leave. You're just making it harder to drag it out.

Go.

'Jenni, I'll write.'

'You do that,' she said formally—dully—lifting her hammer again. 'I guess we'll have a few things to sort out. The divorce and things...'

Her voice died away to nothing. The divorce...

'There's no rush.'

'Not for my sake,' she told him. 'But there's no saying when the urge to remarry might hit you again, William. So you'd best be prepared.'

'I'm not in the market for another wife.'

'No?' She thumped a nail into another shingle with resounding force. 'The marriage profit margin doesn't look good, I guess. Still, you never know. And when opportunity knocks you have to jump right in there, William. Isn't that what being a businessman is all about?'

Her voice cracked with strain, and William took an involuntary step towards the ladder.

'No,' she yelled, and it was a yell of pain. 'Don't you dare come any closer. No!' She shook her head, trying to clear the fog of distress. 'Just go, William. Now. Please. Just go.'

And she lifted another nail and thumped down hard. She missed by a country mile.

Well, what else could she expect when her eyes were filled with tears?

There was one other person William had to visit before he left. He didn't want to, but Jenni's safety depended on it. So, before he finally left Betangera to go to the airport, William found Ronald.

It was difficult to find him. When he went to Martha's old home, the place was boarded up. There was a sign on the front door announcing a mortgage auction to be held in a fortnight.

'You won't find Harbertson there,' a neighbour told William morosely. 'Bailiffs came in yesterday and took everything he owned. They turned off the gas and electricity and water, and they locked him out. He's staying in a hotel, I think.'

He wasn't. William tried the town's hotels, and finally rang the police sergeant. As he suspected, the police knew where he was.

'He's in McAferty's boarding house,' the sergeant told him. 'I don't know how long he'll be there, either.

McAferty's only taken him in because we asked him to, and paid a few days' board. He can't pay his shot after that, and he'll gamble his way through a social services cheque. We figure he'll be out of the town by the end of the week, and it's good riddance.'

'He has no money at all?'

'He gambles and he uses loan sharks,' the policeman said. 'He's in way over his head. There's all sorts of seedy characters after him. He's been holding them off with the promise of the farm, but now that Jenni owns it…' William could almost hear the shrug at the end of phone. 'Well, he's in trouble up to his neck, but he's asked for every inch of it.'

He was indeed in trouble.

It was only five in the afternoon but William found Ronald in bed. The man looked as if he'd been drinking heavily, he hadn't shaved for days and the room was filled with the stale odour of unwashed body and alcohol. He looked up as William came into the room and he practically cringed back under the bedclothes.

'Go to hell,' he told him. 'You've come here to gloat?'

'I'm not here to do anything of the kind,' William told him coldly. He'd hated this man for years. Loathed him. Now, though… The hatred died away. All he felt was an empty, weary distaste. 'I came to tell you I'm leaving. I'm going back to the States.'

That got Ronald's attention. He sat up in bed like a shot, his eyes narrowing.

'You mean… You mean you and that cow aren't sticking it?' He might be so drunk he was incapable of standing, but where money was concerned his mind was sharp as a tack. 'That means…if you don't stay married then that means the farm's mine!'

'No.' William pulled a photocopy of his father's will from his pocket and laid it on the bedside table. 'It doesn't. It means the farm's mine. We found my father's will, Ronald. The farm never has been yours and it's never been your mother's. It's always been mine.'

'What…what the hell do you mean?'

'Read it when I've gone and you'll see.' The quicker he got out of here, the better. The smell in the room was starting to make him feel ill. 'But I've just come to tell you…this is an end to it. There's no way you can touch the farm now, and if I ever find you've hurt Jenni or her sisters in any way I'll kill you. That's a promise. With my own bare hands I'll kill you. You stay away from Jenni and stay away from her sisters and the farm. Is that clear?'

Then, at Ronald's look of absolute bewilderment, he found it in him to feel a twinge of pity.

If anyone had ever told him he'd feel sorry for Ronald, he would have laughed. But now… This pathetic little man had nothing. Nothing!

William sighed, lifted a cheque-book from his pocket and wrote. Then he laid the cheque down on the copy of his father's will.

'Here's ten thousand dollars, Ronald,' he told him. 'I haven't a clue why I'm giving it to you, so don't ask. Use it to pay the worst of your creditors and then get out of here. Start up somewhere. Get yourself a job.'

'What…start with nothing?'

'I did and Jenni did,' William said bleakly. 'You've been given your mother's home and my father's fortune. You've wasted them both. This is your last chance. And if I never see you again after this it'll be too soon.'

He turned then, and walked out of the room—and blotted Ronald from his life for ever.

So why did he feel so empty?

William sat in the departure lounge at the airport and tried to come to terms with what had just happened. Hell, he felt dreadful.

He shouldn't. He was back where he'd started. He had affirmation of his father's love. He'd saved the farm. Jenni and her sisters were secure. Even if they wouldn't accept the farm as a gift, he could make sure they were safe.

He'd achieved everything he'd set out to do, and more.

So why couldn't he get rid of this dreary emptiness?

Jenni…

The vision of her as he'd last seen her flashed into his mind and stayed. Jenni sitting on her roof, battering on shingles. Alone and facing the world head-on.

He should have taken a photograph so he could remember her.

He would remember her. Always. He didn't need any photograph. She was the most beautiful woman. The most wonderful person.

She was his wife…

'Flight 469 to New York boarding from Gate Seven…'

The voice over the loudspeaker started just as the phone in his briefcase began to ring.

He almost didn't answer it. He should have turned it off, he thought. There was no one here to ring him. His mobile telephone had lain unused since the day after the fire.

It kept right on ringing.

It'll be a wrong number, he told himself, but others were staring pointedly at his briefcase as they prepared themselves for boarding. So he took the thing out and flipped it open.

Rachel's fear reached him down the line in a solid, sickening wave.

'William, is that you? Oh, thank God, you haven't left. I… We were just hoping against hope you might have the phone on. William, we can't find Jenni. We think…we think Ronald's taken her. William, come home.'

CHAPTER ELEVEN

TWO a.m.

There was no sleep at Betangera Holiday Cottages. Not even the most hard-hearted of holiday-makers could ignore the police cars, the floodlights, and the obvious distress of Rachel and Beth.

William pulled up between two police cars, ignored the group of strangers and guests, and mounted the verandah steps three at a time.

Rachel met him at the door, flung herself into his arms and sobbed her heart out. The cool, collected university student who knew it all was gone. She was past speaking. She was past anything but sobbing.

As William folded her to him, Beth stood up from the kitchen table with Sam in harness at her side. Her face was ashen. She took two faltering steps forward, and William reached out to take her hand. His free arm was still cradling Rachel to him and he hauled Beth in, too, and held them both. They were kids. Kids!

'What's happening?' he demanded, and if his voice was shaking who could blame him?

It was Beth who told him. Rachel was past speech, but somehow Beth held on to the remnants of coherence.

'He just came and took her,' she told him, in a voice that was filled with tears. 'There was only me here. Rachel had gone for a walk after tea. So he knocked on the door and Jenni answered it. I heard him speak, but I didn't hear what he said. And then...there was a sort of cry and a scuffle.

Sam and I came out, but by the time we reached the door they were gone. I heard a car start up and drive away. Fast.'

The police sergeant came in then. He'd been talking to a couple of officers outside when William had pulled up but William had raced straight past. Now William turned to face him, still holding the girls close.

'Sergeant?'

'I can't tell you much more than Beth's given us,' the police officer said heavily. He put a hand up and ran it through his thinning hair. 'We can't even prove it was Harbertson.'

'They can't prove it because I'm blind,' Beth said dully, and her hand tightened convulsively in William's grasp. 'But it *was* him. I'd know his voice anywhere.'

'He'll have waited until only Beth was here.' The policeman's face was almost as ashen as the girls'. This was a small town and he was taking it hard. 'He'll know...'

Yeah. He'd know. He'd know that Beth's evidence would be weak because she couldn't see. A good defence lawyer could make mincemeat of her.

'He was driving the Jag, though,' William said quickly. 'Maybe... If you put out a search... His car's unmistakable.'

'He wasn't driving the Jaguar,' Beth told him. 'I could pick out the sound of the Jag. It was an older car. An old Holden or a Ford, with a hole in the muffler, I think.'

'Good girl.' That was something, but William's heart still sank. If he was driving an unknown car...

'The Jaguar was repossessed this week, along with the rest of his belongings,' the policeman said. 'We don't know what he was driving. That's one of the things we're working on.'

'But what would he take her for?' Rachel wailed. 'What for?' Her brittle sophistication had left her entirely, and she seemed younger than Beth.

'I don't know,' William said.

But William did know. He remembered the look on Ronald's face as he'd left him. The sick loathing.

Ronald was past reason. The man was past thinking of consequences. He'd lash out at anything he could.

And what he had was Jenni.

William lifted his head and met the police sergeant's eyes across the room, and the bleakness he saw there only confirmed the worst of his fears. The police sergeant knew Ronald, and he knew what he was capable of.

Jenni…

It was the longest night he'd ever known.

Towards three a.m. there was a message for the police. A youth coming out of the local nightclub had just reported his car stolen. It was a fifteen-year-old Holden, its silencer had cracked a week ago and he'd parked it almost directly outside Ronald's boarding house.

At least they knew now what he was driving.

So what? They were now searching for one green, fifteen-year-old Holden, but it could be anywhere. The youth said he had a tank full of petrol. Ronald could be in New South Wales before he had to stop to refill.

With Jenni?

No. Without Jenni. He'd dump her.

But…

Don't let yourself think of that, William told himself. Don't!

More than anything in the world, William wanted to get in his car and go and search. But where? Where?

And Rachel and Beth were clinging to him as if they were drowning. Even Sam pressed his big body against William's, as if drawing comfort from his presence.

Dear God, please…

The police said they had a widening search in place already. William held the girls close and waited. He just had to leave it to them.

He just had to hope.

Four a.m.

The radio on the police sergeant's belt crackled into life. He'd assured William there were scores of police involved in the search now, but the sergeant's task seemed to be to keep William and the girls under his eye.

'I'll stay here in case you get a phone call' he'd said. 'We've tapped your line. Just in case of blackmail,' he'd added—but William was past hoping for that.

Ronald was too far gone to be thinking of blackmail, and he believed William was on his way back to the US. Rachel and Beth had nothing to give as ransom.

Now the policeman lifted his receiver and listened intently. He nodded and grunted.

Then...

'Okay. It'll take time to get men in there, but I want everything you have. Tracker dogs. The lot. Three hours? Okay, if I have to wait three hours I will, but get them here as soon as possible. Now.'

Then he put down the receiver and turned to William. Beside him, Beth and Rachel could hardly breathe.

'We've found the car,' he said heavily. 'Abandoned.'

'Where?' William was aware of his heart, thumping in his chest like a sledgehammer.

'By Bryces Gulf. It's the National Park area. Wilderness, twenty miles east of here. It's virtual rainforest.'

'Why...?'

'The car's just been left,' the police sergeant said heavily. 'The keys are still in the ignition but no one's around. We can only assume he had someone meet him there, or he's hitched a ride.'

'But...but why there?' Beth's voice was a frightened sob.

'Because it's a great place to dump a body,' Rachel whispered. 'Oh, William, I bet that's it.' Her fingers were digging into his arm so hard that later he found she'd made him bleed. 'He's mad. He's evil and now he's completely flipped. I bet he's killed her.'

Half an hour later William pulled the truck off the road beside Ronald's abandoned car. He'd wanted to join the police here by himself, but there was no way he could. Not with Rachel and Beth clinging like limpets.

Dear God, he was responsible for them. He'd never felt so old and so responsible and so...so absolutely terrified.

What the hell was happening? Where was she?

Block out the thought. Block it out.

He glanced sideways at the girls. Rachel was white faced and staring straight ahead into the night, as though her eyes could pierce the unknown, and Beth was clinging to Sam as if her life depended on him.

If they'd telephoned just ten minutes later he would have already boarded the plane, he thought bleakly. He'd be somewhere above the Pacific Ocean, and they'd be facing this on their own.

He couldn't leave them now. Regardless of what happened...

Don't think of that!

But he couldn't leave them. How could he ever have imagined that he could? These kids were his stepmother's sister's children. They were no relation to him at all, and yet he loved them...

They were Jenni's sisters, and he loved Jenni. They were his wife's sisters.

His wife. Jenni.

A ragged sob rose in his throat and it was all he could do to hold it back. To shove the terror aside and somehow get himself out of the truck and face the group of policemen clustered around Ronald's abandoned car.

'What's happening?' he managed, and it was all he could do to get the words out. A senior officer broke away from the group and came across to him.

'You are?'

'William Brand. Jenni…Jenni is my wife. And these are her sisters.'

'I see.' The policeman looked grave and sympathetic all at once, and William's gut churned in fear. 'Well, I'm afraid there's nothing to tell you, sir. There's no one here. Whether Harbertson's taken her on…'

'He'll have stopped here to dump her…'

'We don't know that, sir.'

'No. But why else would he choose such a desolate place?' William looked around at the cluster of policemen. 'Well? Why aren't you searching?'

'We can't,' the policeman said apologetically. 'There's a track here leading down to a creek at the bottom of the gully. We've been along it but it peters out when it hits the water and there's nothing there. If we go off the track we'll be bush-bashing through unknown territory. I'll lose men. So we wait for tracker dogs at dawn.'

'But…' William lifted his face to the sky. It was starting to rain, lightly now—just mist—but he could smell the oppression of thunder in the air. The weather forecast had predicted storms.

'If this rain sets in…won't you lose any scent?'

'It's a risk we have to take, sir,' the policeman said. 'There's no way we can find anything here in the dark, and the bush is almost impenetrable. People have been lost here before.'

'No.' It was Beth, coming up behind them to listen, Sam still harnessed at her side. With her free hand she grabbed William and tugged him urgently. 'No. We can look.'

'I'm afraid we can't, miss.'

'Yes, we can,' she said fiercely. 'Just because it's dark… Sam and I will go. It's dark for me all the time. I can go. There's no way Sam will let me get lost.'

'But…'

'And Sam's better than any sniffer dog,' Beth said firmly. All of a sudden it was the child who was taking control here. Beth, whose whole world had been snatched away from her once… Beth was fighting with everything she possessed to ensure it didn't happen a second time. 'Sam knows,' she said. 'William, you've seen us work together. It's one of the first things I taught him. If I say "Find Jenni," he'll take me straight to her.'

'I don't see it's possible, miss,' the policeman said, but Beth wasn't listening.

'Make them let me, William,' she said urgently. 'Make them.'

'I have torches in the truck,' William said slowly, his eyes on Sam as he thought this through. It was true. He'd seen. This dog knew Jenni almost as well as he knew Beth. If he could…

It was worth a try. Anything was worth a try. 'I'll go,' he said firmly. 'I'll take Sam. Alone if I must, but I'll go.'

'You can't go by yourself, sir. Not into bush like this.' The policeman stared down at Sam, his expression doubtful. As if in answer to his doubts, a fresh spatter of raindrops fell on their faces. They had to move fast or not at all. And Sam looked up at him, intelligence written in his eyes.

'Very well, then,' he said finally. 'It's worth a try. But my men will do this. We have lanterns. We'll take the dog.'

'No. He only works for me and he only works in harness,' Beth said fiercely. 'You'll just confuse him. William, take me to Ronald's car.'

'I'll take Sam, Beth.'

'No,' she said fiercely. 'He works for me!'

William paused. This was a chance. He saw what was in the policeman's face and he knew what was unspoken. If there were horrors waiting to be found, the girls were best out of it. But Beth was right. Sam worked in harness for her, and Beth and Sam could well be Jenni's last chance.

'Let's go, then, Beth,' he said finally—heavily—and he led her to the open door of Ronald's car. 'Put him in. Let him sniff.'

'Okay, Sam.' Beth encouraged the big dog inside the car. 'Okay. Where's Jenni? Sam, find Jenni. Find Jenni.'

And Sam took a few intent sniffs of the car—then a couple more outside the rear passenger door.

And then he put his nose down, checked for a moment as Beth gathered herself ready at his side, his harness in her hand, and he headed for the walking track down to the river.

What followed were thirty minutes of harrowing walking.

They got three quarters of the way down the track before Sam paused. He sniffed, sniffed again, and then veered sideways into thick, dense bush.

'Hell, we'll have to bush-bash,' the sergeant said. 'They can't have gone this way. Wait. This is crazy.'

But one of his men held a lantern high.

'Look here, sir,' he said urgently. 'These twigs have been snapped off at shoulder height and the break's recent. Someone's crashed through here. I think the dog's right.'

'But…why would they go off the track? And why leave

the car?' Rachel said. 'If Ronald was just…just dumping her…then surely he'd just leave her at the bottom of the track and go. I mean…if the car hadn't been parked up the top, then we'd never have looked here. Not in a million years.'

There seemed no reason, and yet Sam was sure.

So they bush-bashed, with Sam sniffing forward and the men hacking a path around and after him.

And finally William could bear the silence no longer.

'Jenni,' he yelled into the darkness. 'Jenni.'

They all took it up then, checking to make sure their yells didn't deflect the dog. Sam, though, was intent on his task. He kept shoving forward, and every time they checked where he was leading they could find bits of broken twig or squashed undergrowth to show the search wasn't stupid.

The mist was becoming wetter, turning to rain. How long could a scent last?

Please…

It was a silent sob echoing drearily in William's heart, while his deep voice echoed out through the bushland.

'Jenni…Jenni…'

And then, as if by magic, there was a faint answering cooee.

At first it was so faint they hardly heard it. Only Beth, her ears tuned to search by sound as other people were tuned to sight, stood stock-still and halted Sam in his progress. William was walking just in front of her, clearing the bush at head height so girl and dog wouldn't be impeded. Now she stood still and gripped William's arm. Hard.

'Listen.'

Nothing.

'Yell again, William,' Beth said urgently, and William did. He cupped his hands and his voice echoed out around them and away into the reaches of the night.

'Jenni…'

And this time it was unmistakable. 'Cooee…' Faint. Quavering. But close. Not more than two hundred yards.

And Sam put his nose down and lurched forward, and Beth and William were running—crashing through the undergrowth and ignoring scratched faces, with the others left behind to follow as best they could.

Jenni was lying under a rocky outcrop, dug in behind a mass of fern and grevillea. The group could have walked straight past her and never found her. But Sam put his belly down on the ground and wriggled forward, his whole body quivering with delight. Beth had to release the harness to let him go where he wanted.

William flung himself down on the ground and hauled himself in behind.

And two seconds later he had her, cradled in his arms and holding her to his heart as if he would never let her go in her life. Or his life.

Not ever.

She was hurt, but she wasn't hurt to death.

The policemen macheted the ferns and grevillea and formed a clearing. Then, somehow, the sergeant prised back the girls and dog, and he and his men lifted William and Jenni clear of Jenni's niche. To separate them was impossible. Where Jenni went, so did William.

'Let's see what gives, sir,' the policeman said gruffly, his voice barely concealing his emotion. They'd known Harbertson and they'd been looking for a tragedy—but Jenni was alive and no one could cling like this if they were near death.

And finally William released her enough so they could

see—so Rachel could step in with her third-year medical training and run trembling hands over her sister.

Her arm was broken and there was a gash just above her breast. It was jagged and bleeding sluggishly.

'But it's not deep,' Rachel said on a sob. 'Oh, Jenni, it's not deep. You'll be okay.'

Jenni didn't answer. She just clung to William with her good arm, and her whole body shook. And William folded her to him once more. Bother pressure pads on her wound. His body would do as well.

What in heaven's name had he ever been thinking of, about to get on a plane back to the States? This was his home. This was his woman.

This was his life, and he'd been given another chance.

'Where's Harbertson?' the sergeant was asking, as if he didn't really expect an answer. Jenni seemed too deeply shocked to speak.

But she did—her voice muffled by William's sweater. By William's love.

'He's somewhere here,' she whispered. 'I think...I think he's lost, too. I heard him crashing around just before you came. I... He's still looking for me.'

'He's here!' William put her back from him then—not much, but a fraction so he could see her face. 'Jenni...'

'He was going to kill me,' she said, and her voice was matter-of-fact. Too matter-of-fact. Her face was deathly white. 'Down at the river. He told me. I think... I think he must be on drugs or something. He was just...mad. He shoved me out of the car and held me, with a knife against my back. He was going to kill me at the river and then throw my body in the water. He kept saying it over and over. But then...'

'You fought him off?' William asked, in a voice that shook. His lips went into her hair. 'Jenni...'

'I could hear the water when we were getting near the river so I knew... I knew he'd kill me soon. He was behind me and the knife was in my back, pushing me forward. But I thought...well, what have I got to lose? So I pretended to stumble. And then I turned and lashed out at him. He...he hit me with the knife and grabbed me by the arm, but I managed to grab the knife and pull away. I threw the knife into the bush, and then I kicked him—just as hard as I could.'

She gave a half sob, half laugh. 'But he was still between me and the track. So I took off into the bush. And he came after me.'

'Jenni...'

'That's all,' she said. 'He's been searching. For a while he was searching for me. But...I ran and ran until I couldn't go any more. Until I thought I was out of his earshot. Then I just lay here. Lay here and waited. After a while I heard him again. But the last time I heard him...he sounded frightened. I think...I think he's lost the track, too.'

'Oh, Jenni...'

But the sergeant was barking into his radio transmitter.

'Get a watch on the car. Get men stationed along the road. We'll wait. If Harbertson comes out, I want him.'

He put a hand on Jenni's uninjured arm. 'You're sure of this, miss? You're sure he intended to kill you?'

'Quite sure,' Jenni said wearily. 'Quite...'

And she looked up at William and sighed. And then her eyes closed, and she slipped into unconsciousness.

CHAPTER TWELVE

SHE'D been here before.

Jenni opened her eyes to see the same walls and door and furniture she'd stared at four weeks before—the night before her wedding.

Hospital. She was in hospital.

She stirred and a jolt of pain shot down her arm. She winced, but before she could stir again a large hand came over from behind her and held her still.

'Hush, Jenni. Don't move. I'll come around the other side.'

He was behind her.

She would have ignored the pain and shifted, but he was too fast. Before she could as much as blink, William was around the other side of the bed, kneeling on the floor and taking her face between his hands.

And kissing her, oh, so gently, on the lips.

'My Jenni,' he said, and all the joy of the morning was in his voice. 'My love.'

'Will…William.' Her voice was a thready whisper. 'How long have you been here?'

'Since we brought you in last night.' He glanced at his watch. 'About eight hours ago. Do you remember?'

'Not very much.' She forced her fuzzy mind back, but the details were sketchy.

She remembered vaguely coming around in the police car and finding William cradling her close, and then drifting in and out of consciousness during the long ride to hospital.

She vaguely remembered white coats and people talking of stitches and setting her arm—and bright lights over her head.

And William, always there. William.

'Beth…Rachel…' she whispered.

'They've gone home to sleep. They could see you were safe. They're fine.'

'And…and Ronald?'

'He's in jail.' William's smile caressed her. It enveloped her in its tenderness, and it took her breath away. 'He could hear us shouting in the bush. When we started bush-bashing our way out, he realised that without us he was hopelessly lost. That bushland can swallow a man up, never to be seen again. In the end, he yelled to us to wait, and he came out.'

'So you rescued him, too.'

'Not because I wanted to,' William told her. 'But there's enough evidence now to lock him up for a good few years.' He touched the dressing on her shoulder and the smile on his face faded. 'Bastard…'

'Don't…'

'I've never been so afraid in my life,' he told her, and he put his face down to kiss her hair. He let his head rest there. 'Oh, Jenni… They rang me at the airport and told me he had you. And I'd seen Harbertson. I'd seen what condition he was in. I should have guessed.'

'You'd never guess anyone could be capable of that.'

'No. But…' He shook his head, shaking off a nightmare. 'If it wasn't for your courage… And Beth and Sam…'

'They found me?'

'They did.' William's smile returned in full. 'It's the only good thing that's come of all this. It started pelting with rain twenty minutes after we found you. Without Beth and Sam, you'd still be in the bush. Where you were….even if Ronald didn't find you, with the loss of blood and shock and pain… By morning…'

He closed his eyes and then forced them open again, as if making sure she was still there.

'And it was down to Beth,' he told her. 'Beth knows that. If she wasn't blind and if she didn't have the best seeing-eye dog in the world, then we would have lost you, Jenni. Just now, she told me she felt like she's been given the world. Not just you, Jenni. But she's been given back her dignity. Her place in the sun. You won't stop her now. There's nothing that kid can't do.'

'I'm so glad...' Jenni's voice faded to a whisper and William gathered her to him and held her.

'You're done in, sweetheart. You need to sleep.'

'No.' Her eyes opened again, and her fingers came out to touch his shirt-front. 'William...'

'Yes, love?'

'When I wake up again...will you still be here?'

Silence.

For a long, long moment there was nothing between them but silence. Nothing.

And then, slowly, tenderly and with infinite love, William gathered his wife to him. Heart against heart.

'I'll be here, Jenni. I'll always be here.'

'William...'

'No. Hush. Let me speak.' He placed his fingers on her lips and then ran his hand through her hair. Wonderingly. As if, even now he couldn't believe she'd been restored to him.

'Jenni, I've been every sort of fool,' he told her. 'Since I was eighteen I cut emotion right out of my life. It was like I couldn't afford to let myself feel. I was so hurt! And then, when I was twenty-six, I came up for air from my solitary life of making money—making myself so financially secure nothing could touch me—and I met Julia. For just a while there I thought I could rebuild something. Only it was stupid.

I got shot down in flames again. So I went back to making money, and using people for what I could get out of them.'

'William, don't...'

'I need to say this to you, Jenni,' he said softly. 'I know you're tired but... Dear heaven, all last night I thought this through, and I thought I'd never be able to say it to you. But now... You're here. You're alive.' And he bent and kissed her full on the lips.

'Jenni, I love you,' he told her, when finally he paused to give her breath. And Jenni just had to see his face to know that what he spoke was the truth. 'You're my family. My heart. I love Beth and I love Rachel and I love Sam, but most of all—most of all I love you. You've taught me what it's like to be a human again. You've hauled me out of my bank vault and you've made me live. I didn't see it. I came so close to going back to the States, without seeing that what you were offering was worth more than all the gold in the universe. Jenni, you're the most beautiful...the bravest...the kindest...'

Jenni's eyes closed again. She was weak past belief. She was tired and filled with pain, and the effects of the anaesthetic and last night's horrors were still with her. But somewhere inside her heart was filled to bursting. Filled with love and hope and desire. And joy. All the joy in the world.

'Jenni, give me another chance,' William said, and his voice was urgent. 'You must. Jenni, I love you. I want you. More than anything else in the world, I want to marry you again. Properly this time, with vows that mean for ever. You must, Jenni. Please, my love. You must.'

And Jenni's good arm came slowly up from under the bedclothes, and her fingers caught around her lover's face and pulled him to her. So that his lips met hers. So that she could feel his warmth. His touch. His being.

'Oh, my love,' she whispered. 'My heart. My William.

Of course I must. Of course I must love you. I will for a lifetime.'

It was sunset on Betangera Beach.

Six weeks had passed since Jenni had been hurt. She still wore a light plaster on her forearm but it no longer bothered her. The long, jagged cut was now a fading scar.

Ronald was behind bars and would stay that way for years.

William had stayed for a week after Jenni came home from hospital—enough time to start a small army of people working at the cottages. Jenni now had cleaners and carpenters and painters at her beck and call, and the cottages had never looked better.

William had flown to the States and closed down his central office.

'We're an international corporation now,' he'd told an astonished Harriet. 'With e-mail and faxes and teleconferencing, we can keep this chain going from anywhere in the world. I'm running my end from Betangera. You and Walter are my front people here. Do you want to stay in New York, or would you like to base yourselves somewhere else?'

And Walter and Harriet had looked at each other, astounded.

'You mean—anywhere?' Harriet had asked.

'As long as your choice has electricity and a telephone.'

'Well…' Walter, fifty and balding and four years on from his first wife's death, had looked for a long time at Harriet. And a slow smile had dawned.

'If I keep being administrator for this corporation for the next ten years, I wouldn't mind fitting in some fishing on the side,' he said. 'How about it, Harriet? Can you bait a hook? How about we head to the mountains? Together.'

And Harriet had blushed a deep shade of pink and stammered and giggled like a schoolgirl.

The thing had been settled. They'd come to the city if necessary—but then so would William. If absolutely necessary, he'd fly back to the States, with Jenni by his side.

'Because where I go she goes,' he'd growled, and Harriet had giggled again, and blushed, and Walter had held her around the waist as if he'd just found a treasure. Good grief! Was love contagious?

And then William had flown back to Betangera.

'You'll be bored out of your brain,' his friends had told him, but William didn't think so.

'I'll set up the best restaurant you've ever seen, right in the midst of our cottages,' he'd said. 'Tiny and exclusive and only available to house guests. What's the bet we'll have an international five-star rating within a year?'

And no one who'd seen the determination in his eyes had been able to doubt him.

And then he was back with his Jenni.

Back to a wedding.

Now they stood, hand in hand, where the tongues of foam licked the golden sand before rushing back to gain strength for another try. The sun was slipping over the mountains, a vast golden ball casting its fiery hue over the sea. The sand was still sun-warmed from the day.

The scene was magic.

The bride stood bare-toed and clad in jeans and T-shirt, with her hair braided.

'Because that's how I first saw you,' William told her. 'That's how I love you.'

'You didn't like my bridal finery?'

'I loved your bridal finery,' he said firmly. 'I'm so in love with you that I even love your No Brand knickers. But I love you best in this.'

'Well, you're one up on me,' Jenni told him, kissing him long and lovingly on the mouth, 'because I love you best in nothing at all...'

William groaned and somehow dragged his attention back to the matter in hand. To the celebrant waiting to marry them for the second time. To Beth and Rachel and Sam—their only witnesses to this private exchange of the very deepest of vows.

'With this ring I thee wed. With my body I thee worship. With all my worldly goods I thee endow... That means pigs,' Jenni said as William caught her face in his hands and bent to kiss her. 'The pigs are yours, my love.'

'How about the satin sheets?'

'You can have them, too,' Jenni told him. 'I don't want them.'

'I have news for you, Mrs Brand,' Mr Brand told her. 'For your wedding gift I've bought you silk ones. Silk sheets.'

'Silk sheets...' Jenni gasped. 'You didn't.'

'I did.'

'All for me?'

'Nope,' he told her as he pulled her back into his arms. 'You've just made a vow. "With all my worldly goods I thee endow." You've just given 'em back to me. So...we'll just have to share. Now, how are we going to do that, my love, my heart?'

'We could cut them in half?'

'We could.' He appeared to consider. 'Or...one each?'

'Or...'

'Or we could sleep in them,' William told her as the first evening star appeared low on the horizon. Rachel, Beth and Sam stood by with three identical expressions of dopey satisfaction on their faces.

As two people became one.

'We can sleep in them together,' William told her. 'Together, my love. For ever.'

'We'll wear them out.'

'Let's try.'

FREE!

4 Books
and a surprise gift!

We would like to take this opportunity to thank you for reading this Mills & Boon® book by offering you the chance to take FOUR more specially selected titles from the Enchanted™ series absolutely FREE! We're also making this offer to introduce you to the benefits of the Reader Service™ —

★ FREE home delivery
★ FREE gifts and competitions
★ FREE monthly Newsletter
★ Books available before they're in the shops
★ Exclusive Reader Service discounts

Accepting these FREE books and gift places you under no obligation to buy; you may cancel at any time, even after receiving your free shipment. Simply complete your details below and return the entire page to the address below. **You don't even need a stamp!**

YES! Please send me 4 free Enchanted books and a surprise gift. I understand that unless you hear from me, I will receive 6 superb new titles every month for just £2.40 each, postage and packing free. I am under no obligation to purchase any books and may cancel my subscription at any time. The free books and gift will be mine to keep in any case.

N9EB

Ms/Mrs/Miss/Mr ....Initials ....

BLOCK CAPITALS PLEASE

Surname...

Address...

....

....Postcode ....

Send this whole page to:
THE READER SERVICE, FREEPOST CN81, CROYDON, CR9 3WZ
(Eire readers please send coupon to: P.O. Box 4546, DUBLIN 24.)

mps MAILING PREFERENCE SERVICE